Bringing Tony Home

Also by Tissa Abeysekara

In the Kingdom of the Sun and the Holy Peak
Pitagamkarayo
Roots, Reflections & Reminiscences

Bringing Tony Home

Stories by
Tissa Abeysekara

North Atlantic Books
Berkeley, California

Scala House Press
Seattle, Washington

Published by
North Atlantic Books   Scala House Press
P.O. Box 12327   P.O. Box 4518
Berkeley, California 94712   Seattle, Washington 98194

Cover photos: Buddhist statue Sri Lanka © Jean-Claude Gallard, istockphoto; dog © Valery Shanin, Big Stock Photo
Cover design © Paula Morrison
Book design © Ayelet Maida, A/M Studios
Printed in the United States of America

Bringing Tony Home is sponsored by the Society for the Study of Native Arts and Sciences, a nonprofit educational corporation whose goals are to develop an educational and cross-cultural perspective linking various scientific, social, and artistic fields; to nurture a holistic view of arts, sciences, humanities, and healing; and to publish and distribute literature on the relationship of mind, body, and nature.

North Atlantic Books' publications are available through most bookstores. For further information, call 800-733-3000 or visit our website at www.north atlanticbooks.com.

Library of Congress Cataloging-in-Publication Data
Abesekara, Tissa
    Bringing Tony home : stories / by Tissa Abeysekara.
        p. cm.
    Summary: "Part memoir and part fiction, this collection of stories provides a historically compelling portrait of a young boy's childhood and coming of age in Sri Lanka in the 1940's and 1950's"—Provided by publisher.
    ISBN 978-1-55643-757-1
    1. Sri Lanka—Fiction. I. Title.
    PR9440.9.A23B76 2008
    823'.914—dc22
                                          2008026580

1 2 3 4 5 6 7 8 9 SHERIDAN 14 13 12 11 10 09 08

To Lester James Peries:
guide, guru, and friend at all times in most things

Contents

In front of the barn a woman held a duck whose throat she had cut and stroked him gently while a little girl held up a cup to catch the blood for making gravy. The duck seemed very contented and when they put him down (the blood all in the cup) he waddled twice and found that he was dead. We ate him later, stuffed and roasted; and many other dishes, with the wine of that year and the year before and the great year four years before that and other years that I lost track of . . .

— Ernest Hemingway, *Death in the Afternoon*

❦

"If I die and am born again as you say I will be, is that, which is reborn, the same me?" queried the man from the Buddha, and the Buddha replied, "Neither you, nor yet any other."

Likewise, what follows in this book, being truth recreated through memory, is neither true, nor untrue. But then, does it matter?

Bringing Tony Home

—

A Story in Three Movements

The Sunset

It was twilight on a day in early March 1996, but the sun was still big and red like it is from November through February as it dipped over the skyline, and I drove out of the Television Training Institute premises and swung right towards Independence Square, and on my left through the fir trees, lining the old race course, there were glimpses of a red sky.

Camera tracks parallel Gunapala as he moves slowly across the paddy field, bare after the harvest and full of pools of water reflecting the evening light. The main musical theme played by the horanewa emerges on the soundtrack, faintly at first like from a great distance, and increases in volume. Gunapala stops and the camera stops with him, framing the full expanse of the stubble field stretching across the Kesbewa Highway towards Bellanwila, and beyond that the sky, vast and awesomely red and rising in a great big arc over the Attidiya marshes. As the camera stops, the white car bearing Missie Nona away from the village enters frame right on the road that cuts across the field in mid-center distance running parallel to the main highway, and the strings come on the track backing the horanewa building up into a big orchestral score, and then the camera begins to crane up, all this happening at once.

I was now moving away from the setting sun, along Baudd-dhaloka Mawahta, passing the BMICH and towards the General Cemetery, and ahead of me it was already dark under the giant mara trees, and traffic was moving leisurely, homeward bound.

The craning movement of the camera stops. The white car stops, halfway across frame. On the soundtrack there is a pause in the orchestral buildup. Then from deep within the orchestra comes the piercing cry of the esraj, spiraling upwards in a long looping bar.

Sir Oliver Goonetilleke's statue at the Castle Street round-about zoomed forward slowly in silhouette. The esraj continued its heartrending cry as I moved around the statue and straightened towards Sri Jayawardenapura. *The white car has started moving again, right to left. The strings come again, drowning the esraj and building up in volume. White car exits frame, left. Gunapala turns back and walks slowly, head downcast. He disappears down bottom frame. The blood red of the sky is paling now, and traffic is flowing along the main road far away, the vehicles hardly discernible from the darkening foliage at the bottom of the sky.*

Then the whistle of the Kelani Valley train wafts gently over the scene like the cry of a lone bird, indescribably sad.

That was the end of *Pitagamkarayo*—English title: *The Outsiders*—my twelve-hour-long television series—and on that day in March, I was going home after completing the final episode, sound dub, titles, and all. My mind was crosscutting between reality and the last moments of the film I had just completed in the editing room. It had taken exactly two years from the first day of shooting to the end of postproduction. Now the master tapes were ready to be delivered to the client, and the telecast was scheduled to begin on the 9th of April.

That complicated shot, which closes the series, was the first to be recorded. It was on 26 February 1994. The scene was staged on the vast paddy field beginning at the edge of an embankment below the High Level Road, opposite the Nawinna Railway Station—now obscured by the Arpico showroom—and sprawling all the way past Bellanwila Temple towards the Attidiya marshes. On its way the paddy field surrounds on three sides the village of Egodawatta, a place I arrived in as a ten-year-old boy and that was home to me for well over two decades until I left it at the tail end of my youth, and which provided me with the dramatic and emotional backdrop for the narrative in *Pitagamkarayo*.

Growing up in Egodawatta, first as a lonely boy and then

as a wayward teenager, I had watched, fascinated, the awesome sunset over Attidiya many a time. Now almost three decades later, I had returned to capture it on film.

The scene required precise timing of the action blending with camera movement, and the crew and production team of thirty people—quite a large one for Sri Lankan filmmaking—had slaved and struggled the whole afternoon in the blazing sun, rehearsing, perfecting every detail, and making sure we could roll the camera when the sky was right.

The byroad crossing the paddy field and linking Egodawatta with a main macadam road half a mile ahead—two decades ago only a "niyara" broader than the rest and just wide enough for two people to pass—now contains a fair amount of traffic at this hour. It's a shortcut to the provincial town of Boralesgamuwa for motorists coming from Colombo and its south suburbs, and I wanted it closed for the shot. The white car should be the single moving object; any other would disturb, distract. On the little culvert spanning the canal flowing across the field at right angles to the road, I had placed two men winnowing paddy.

It was nearly six thirty in the evening, almost nightfall, when the fourth take was over, and we called it a day. Next morning we were moving to Padukka to settle down for an unbroken shooting schedule of three months when we hoped to wrap it up.

A journey long awaited had at last begun, and like a bunch of schoolkids on the eve of a difficult hill climb, we were excited.

It turned out to be a long march.

The shooting of *Pitagamkarayo* was a prolonged nightmare, and there were many moments in the crisis-ridden production when its completion was seriously in doubt. Finally when it did end on that March evening, it was almost a miracle, and I should have been mightily relieved. But as I drove home I felt disoriented, like when coming out of a coma. *Pitagamkarayo*, like a drug, had got into my bloodstream, and both within and without I was in a twilight zone.

For the next couple of weeks I moved around as if in a dream and I lingered on in a world of memories and shadows. My mind was a confusing montage of images constantly crosscutting between past and present, fantasy and fact. Through it all there was a recurring motif. It was an episode from my childhood over forty years back in time, something which was always there in my memory as clearly as if it happened yesterday. But now it kept coming back with an intensity I had never felt before.

In the last years of the forties, when I had still not reached ten years of age, my family became desperately poor. My parents were very middle-class people from Colombo suburbia who for a very special personal reason had settled down in the village of Depanama, twelve miles up the Kelani Valley railroad and bordered by the lush green paddy fields of Hokandara. We lived in splendid isolation in a large house built just on the eve of the war on land that sloped down from a macadam road—which began at the Pannipitiya Railway Station and proceeded to Borella, one of the better known suburbs of Colombo—to the paddy fields, and the house was of split level where from the upper level one could drive out into the road, and if you descended a flight of steps to the lower level you could walk through a spacious back garden all the way to the paddy fields and beyond, where on some days just above the thin line of hazy-green vegetation you could see Sri Pada, the Holy Peak, like a single brush stroke on the blue sky.

Then a few years after, the war disaster struck in the form of a financial implosion—now that's another story.

In the year 1950, we were moving house for the second time within two years, having moved once before to a smaller house from the big one in the same vicinity. Now we were moving out of the area completely, and by some strange coincidence the month was March once again, as faithfully recorded in Father's diary.

Tony

We, Mother carrying Sister, and I, left Depanama when it was just beginning to get dark. We walked up the narrow gravel path on to the Pannipitiya-Borella Road, passed Ambagashatara Handiya—the junction of the four mango trees—with the man at the boutique trying to light his old Petromax lamp and Mother hurrying past because she didn't want to be explaining things to him, perhaps; then as we took the bend near Manchi Akka's little tea boutique opposite the gate leading to the village headman's house, the Kelani Valley train was pulling out of the Pannipitiya Railway Station, the little compartments already lit and moving in a chain like a glowworm seen over the low line of cactus bushes on the edge of the embankment beyond which rose the two-story building of the station, and the sad whistle of the train rose and fell three times, lingered in the air, and then settled over everything.

Tony, our dog who had been with us for well over seven years, followed us all the way, and packs of vicious mongrels came snarling and howling and he defied them all, swinging deftly every which way with a short clipped bark full of disdain for the hoi polloi. We crossed over from the Old Road beyond the railway station, through an ancient gatepost fallen on its side like some historic ruin and which would have stood there long before the High Level Road came and severed it from a large coconut estate, and now we came to a spot on the "Alut Para"—no one then called it the High Level Road, for the new road to Avissawella had to be identified in relation to the old road—and waited for the bus to take us to Wijerama Junction, five miles towards Colombo.

The suitcase Mother carried in one hand and the reed bag—pan malla, which I carried and which smelled of onions and milchard rice—were deposited on the ground and Tony settled down among them, panting happily and giving us grateful looks, for he was never allowed to follow us this far from home. I squatted by his side in the gloom of late evening, and felt him warm, and my fingers were moving through the soft light-brown coat, and I kissed him lightly on the forehead and there was a quick movement of the muzzle touching my cheek. He smelled good. Tony always smelled good, even after we became poor and could not care for him like before and he was constantly away, moving with stray dogs, over the fields and under the rubber trees, through the scrub jungle, but always at home in the evening, and never smelling bad, looking clean like when we were at the big house and he was sent out only at the end of a leash led by a servant.

Now it was dark at the bus stop, dark enough for lights, but the bus came without headlamps, emerging slowly out of the late evening shadows, preceded by a mighty roar and rattle. It was one of those low-roofed open-bodied affairs with two seats up front next to the driver and two rows next entered by two openings on either side and at the back two rows facing each other with two seats back-to-back in the middle where there was a metal pole holding the roof and with a rear entrance with a two-step footboard on which the conductor usually rode.

We got in from the rear entrance and Tony was awaiting his turn impatiently, placing his paw twice on the footboard to be pushed back by the conductor. "Chip chip," said the conductor never even looking fully at the dog, and I was too frightened to look back as I sat away from Mother in a seat on the side row and kept looking past the driver's head and through the slightly upturned half-of-a-windscreen to the darkness beyond, until I heard the conductor shout "Raaaaaights" and the bus lurched forward with a shudder and the headlamps came suddenly, piercing the dark in a yellow shaft of light.

Our new home was half a house in the village of Egodawatta and at that time was reached only by a gravel path that skirted an RAF camp on the right and an expanse of shrub land broken by a couple of thatched huts on the other, and which in turn gave way to a plot of rubber, dark and gloomy even at high noon. The village began at the end of the rubber plot and sloped gently through old homesteads strewn all around with straw and cow dung and dark and damp under coconut, jak, breadfruit, and all kinds of other trees, and ended in the paddy fields on all three sides. The narrow cart track to the village branched off from a broader road that began at the Wijerama Junction just within sight of the eighth mile post on the High Level Road, moved through a middle-class residential area of neat houses with glass-paned windows and parapet walls and well-kept little gardens heavy with roses, crotons, and bougainvillea, crested a hill coming into full view of the British RAF camp—this is the site of the present Sri Jayawardenapura University—which occupied both sides of the road save one block of land with three attached houses first, with their narrow and half-enclosed verandas opening out onto the road, and then a fairly large house set deep inside a garden with a parapet wall with two gates— one permanently closed—and took an abrupt elbow bend to the right and once again cutting through the camp premises proceeded to Rattanapitiya—a small junction on the Colombo-Kesbewa Highway.

The cart track to Egodawatta at this elbow bend moved along one border of the camp, fenced by tall concrete columns with their top ends tilting outwards and holding thick coils of barbed wire. At regular intervals were tall mahogany trunks rising above the concrete columns and holding a large electric bulb with a plain shade with a broad rim.

Night had fallen when I first walked this stretch with Mother, all the way from Wijerama to Egodawatta. Father had gone before with the single bullock cart that held all the worldly belongings we were now left with. Mother was carrying my sister, two years old then, and she (Mother) held the suitcase in one hand. I carried the pan malla smelling of onions and milchard rice.

I was sad and I was angry. Not because we had left Depanama. Not because we had become poor and were shifting to half a house; I was too young to understand the implications of that, and I was not angry because I was carrying a bag full of smelly onions and milchard rice.

I was sad and angry because we had left Tony behind.

Four days later I was back at Depanama, alighting from a near-empty bus and walking along the road above the railway line where the tips of the cactus bushes on the embankment were still wet with dew and the eight o'clock sun warm on the flower pots hanging from the scalloped roof-edge of the little veranda of the Morawaka dispensary, the red, pink, yellow, and purple flowers dripping over in thick clusters.

I was sent with some specific things to do: buy the weekly rations from the co-op store, collect the new ration books from the headman's office, and also, if I could feel up to it, collect the dressing table mirror—now the mirror was part of the old ebony dressing table, one of the few items left over from the days at the big house, and Mother didn't want to risk getting it cracked in transport, and she detached it from the table and left it at Mr. Lawrence Perera's house—he was our immediate neighbor, worked at Cargills and wore a full suit complete with tie, was Catholic, and went to church every Sunday with his family, and in their house was a gramophone, which played the latest songs of Ananda Samarakoon, and the eldest boy, Anton, was my best friend—to be collected later. But I had another very important task to perform, something I had secretly vowed to myself I would do.

I WAS GOING TO TAKE TONY HOME. WALK WITH HIM ALL THE WAY FROM DEPANAMA TO EGODAWATTA.

Now I walked past Manchi Akka's boutique, and up the little rise in the macadam road to Ambagashatara, the Four Mango Trees, only two were there when I came to know the place, or as I remember it, two gnarled fruitless giants—and began to proceed on the left of the road bordering Mrs. Jayasinghe's land, and through the thickly leafy veralu trees bunched together by the edge of the road I could see the sun bright on the open patch where once stood the tennis court, and where cattle would lie now at all times of the day and especially at high noon, sunning themselves, sprawled like carcasses, very still, with crows on them picking ticks. The veralu trees were in full bloom, and the canopies were flecked with white, and all along that side of the road the flowers lay scattered, thin pale white pieces like shredded strings, and the air was heavy with that strange scent of veralu flowers—a smell that was vaguely familiar and disturbing at the same time—something that also belonged somewhere else but that I couldn't quite place then.

The smell followed me after I passed the trees and came up to the spot where there was a break in the thick undergrowth along the edge of Mrs. Jayasinghe's land. Here I could still see traces of the old driveway leading up to the house, and the empty space where once the house stood, leading me quickly in a jump-cut in time to one of my earliest memories when we had dinner in that house, and Mrs. Jayasinghe—a rotund lady with short-cropped hair and who was Burgher but who wore a sari because she was married to Mr. Jayasinghe who was Sinhala—had placed me on her lap and was trying to make me eat some pudding because Mother couldn't make me eat it, and Uncle

Ronald—Mrs. Jayasinghe's eldest son—was playing an accordion. Only the visual came with no sound, like when the soundtrack of a movie is switched off.

And then came the bark; the sharp clipped aristocratic bark, and with it came Tony, crashing through Mrs. Jayasinghe with the custard pudding in the dessert cup held delicately in one hand and the dessert spoon suspended somewhere between my mouth and her ample bosom, and Uncle Ronald opening and closing the folds of the accordion in an arc just below his chin. Tony came out of nowhere, charging and barking, leaping-turning-twisting-rolling-jumping-licking-whining-moaning in a delirium.

By eleven o'clock I had finished all my assignments: rations from the co-op store—the smelly yellowy big-grained milchard, six chundus of it at two per coupon; sugar, brown sticky and smelling faintly like stale bees' honey, three pounds of it; dhal, the variety referred to as "Mysoor parippu," fine-grained and pink and mistakenly believed to be coming from Mysore in India and boycotted under the orders of the JVP when the Indian Peace Keeping Force was alleged to be raping girls in Jaffna in the late eighties until someone enlightened us that the dhal had nothing to do with India and was really "Masoor dhal," which came from Turkey; and wheat flour, finely powdered and called "Amerikkan piti" with a stress on the first k, which implied, of course, that the flour came from America though it may have come from any country where wheat was grown; new ration books from the village headman's office—this time the books were a light blue in color with the smell of fresh biscuits about them; and now I was at Mr. Lawrence Perera's house to collect the mirror.

Tony was faithfully by my side; since that reunion near the entrance to Mrs. Jayasinghe's land he had kept close to me almost desperately not wanting to lose contact again, even ignoring the bun I bought for him though it looked quite certain to me that he had been starving in the last few days.

Fiendish barking and howling had erupted every now and then as we moved through foreign territory but had subsided when we kept going, and Tony kept as close to me as possible, pressing against my legs to reassure himself that I was there with him.

Mr. Perera had gone to work at Cargills, his son Anton, my friend, had gone to school with his two sisters—in fact all the children of the area were at some school somewhere because it was a weekday, and I had not gone to school because I had never gone to school and at that time I was still not going to school—and that's another story—and on that day it suited me fine that none of the kids I knew were at home, because when you have a secret plan you don't want to meet anybody—and Mrs. Perera was trying to persuade me to eat something by way of lunch because it was close to midday, and I was eager to get away because when you have a secret plan you want to keep moving all the time, and Mrs. Perera kept asking me what I was going to do with the dog and I kept improvising a story that Father was going to come within the next few days in Uncle Eugene's car to take him away and Mrs. Perera looked like she didn't believe one word of what I said and I felt she thought we were never going to take the dog away but I was not going to tell her that I intended walking all the way to Egodawatta with the dog because then she would have certainly stopped me from doing such a darned fool thing.

It was very near high noon as I clambered up an embankment and reached the High Level Road, panting, sweating and already feeling exhausted having walked the first near half-a-mile. I avoided going through the old gateposts on the old road just after the level crossing but walked along the road past the post office—now the post office was the front room adjoining the veranda of an old house within a large garden, with the window of the room expanded to form a counter—beyond which on the same side the road fell away to a narrow valley and came up on the other side to meet the High Level Road, and I took the little footpath that linked the two roads, old and new, across the narrow little valley.

On my left hand I carried the mirror—it seemed much heavier and larger than I thought it to be—on the right hand the provisions contained in a gunny bag, and since both my hands were full and I didn't want Tony to stray too much away from me or tarry a while sniffing and peeing, I had him on a thin coir rope with one end tied to my trouser buckle; those days trousers—short as well as long—had two buckles of white nickel on the sides to hold them tight at the waist.

The "Alut Para" was a pretty lonely stretch up to Maharagama in those days and there were no people about when I appeared at a point just before the eleventh mile post where the road cut through a ridge with the land rising steeply on either side in walls of brick-red kapok. The road was a shiny path, looking fresh and clean like it had been washed, as it stretched before me, and I knew it led straight to where I was going—no branching off, no byroads, no risk of taking the wrong turn, and I felt comfortable, like someone was holding my hand.

I walked and I stopped—sometimes to adjust my burdens and sometimes to ease the growing pains in my hands and legs—and after a long time of walking and stopping I reached the spot that is known by a large two-story store with intricate trelliswork in blue and white—Roslin Nonage Kade/Roslin Nona's Boutique—where there was a large mara tree and a gravel road branched off to the left and on the right the same gravel road moved to cross the railway line to meet the old road. Now this would have been a wonderful place to rest a while—it was cool under the shade of the giant mara tree—but there were people at the boutique and I kept moving on and the road sloped down gently across a paddy field, which stretched far away to the left, and there was a little temple at the bottom of the road by the edge of the field and on the right of the road the paddy field continued until it reached the rail track. At the end of the slope in the road and before it started climbing again there were mara trees on either side and this is where I stopped. I virtually collapsed. I was still far away from home, and behind me I could still see the road coming out of the cleft in the ridge at the eleventh mile post.

As I looked around things were blurred, and there was a feeling somewhere in me of getting choked, of not being able to breathe, and my legs were numb and my body wet and slowly going cold, and since this is exactly how I felt when I used to get those fits long ago, and which was the reason I was not sent to school—or rather one of the reasons—I was gripped with fear, which made me sweat more and feel dizzy. Then the thought occurred to me—not in a blinding flash, but in a slow gradual manner like when you slip into a coma, which happened whenever I had those fits, and which is painless because it means giving up the struggle and relaxing—that I will never make it home. I dropped my head on the gunny bag and felt comfortable and I closed my eyes and heard Tony's heavy breathing and felt his breath on my face, and a breeze came over the paddy fields making me cool like when Mother spread a piece of cloth dipped in cologne on my forehead during a high fever.

There was a time lapse here, a slow mix like in a movie, and then I was moving again—not with any conscious effort but just moving like a sleepwalker—pushed or pulled by some atavistic fear, because suddenly the thought of night falling had occurred. The heat of the high noon had dropped, the sky had gone gray, and the smell of rain hung in the air, which moved around silently and stealthily like a cat. The slow climb from under the mara trees was over; the old road joined the new road and the rail track that came along with the old road suddenly pulled away and disappeared among the thick foliage in the large home-gardens behind old houses with sloping roofs and open verandas that once-upon-a-time would have stood far behind their fences but were now almost flush with the new road; a little further up, the old road reappeared, but now it was on the left of the new road and there was only a thin strip of bare land between the two roads and along the old road front were little old houses set inside little plots of land and there was a boutique with a long veranda half enclosed by a counter painted in alternate stripes of blue and white on which were bottles with multicolored lozenges in them; and I kept moving in a daze with hands straining feet paining knees hurting but Tony trotting by my side cool and easy and from somewhere over and beyond the tangle of coconut tree tops and sloping roofs on my right came the sad and melancholy whistle of the Little Train.

Then there was the little house by the edge of the road — it stood and still stands, a good forty-five years later — just after a point where the old road merges with the new road to re-emerge separately on the other side — the right once more — and just before the new road (then) ran bordering an abandoned rubber plantation with an old upstair house set deep inside. The little house stood very near the road and it had a small open veranda over which the roof sloped down to rest on four thin wooden columns painted a brick red. There was a teapoy in the middle of the veranda with a tablecloth, white and tasseled at the edges, and on the table was a brass bowl mounted on three brass elephants with raised trunks. There were two chairs with armrests placed against the wall and on the wall just above the backs of the chairs were two framed rabbits facing each other, and the rabbits were made of satin cloth molded inside with cotton in bas-relief and outlined with colored beads and sequins —I couldn't see all these details from the road but knew them by memory because the identical handiwork decorated the main doorway of Geera Atha's house—and Geera Atha was a very old man who brought us milk every morning, and lived all by himself in a very old house that stood at the end of the gravel road a little beyond Mr. Lawrence Perera's homestead.

The two rabbits on the wall facing each other in the little house by the road pulled me out of the trancelike state in which I was walking; it was something like coming out of a tunnel, or like when you have strayed too far out and you hear something or smell something or see something and you know you're still within reach and not lost.

I stopped. Right in front of the house. And all of a sudden I felt thirsty. I must have been thirsty all along, but now looking fondly at the two rabbits on the wall I wanted a drink of water very badly.

Putting down the things in my hands was in slow motion, because the hands had gone stiff under the weight and took time to move. The gunny bag, stiff and bulging with the provisions, stood upright on the ground and the mirror was placed on its face against the bag and Tony, released for a moment from my waist, first sat on his hind legs and then stretched himself full length from paw to tail-end panting and drooling at the mouth but looking quite pleased with himself. My eyes moved casually over the bag and I had the feeling that something was amiss, but I couldn't quite place my finger on it. I put my hand inside the bag and felt the rice and the two packs containing sugar and dhal and my hand began to smell of milchard but still I had that uneasy feeling that something was missing and then all at once it struck like a thunderbolt: the ration books. The ration books were missing. My knees felt as if they were melting and a hot lump rose up from the guts and pressed against the chest, and it made me dizzy in the head and now I was feeling cold all over like when I used to get those fits.

(In those days the ration book was an important article in one's existence; it was legal evidence of Ceylonese — Sri Lanka was Ceylon then — citizenship and carried with it the right of universal franchise — and that was crucial when the first UNP government of independent Ceylon headed by Mr. D.S. Senanayake was busy denying segments of Indian labor on the plantations Ceylonese citizenship and deporting them to India — it was the national identity card, and if you happened to be poor, like what we had become, was the sole means of your weekly subsistence all rolled into one; without the ration book you were a nonperson, and if you lost it the procedure to obtain a new one was very complicated, involving affidavits, long hours at the DRO's office, etc, and once a servant — that is when we were at the big house — lost Father's book and he was mad having to go through all the trouble of getting a new one and swore that's the last time he will go through the procedure and warned Mother to be careful in future, and Mother was so very careful — especially after we became poor and kept it locked in her little almirah — and now I had gone and lost not one book but all four, which meant the entire family was wiped out from Ceylon in one fell blow, and that by me doing a damn fool thing — walking with a stupid dog all the way from Depanama.)

IT CERTAINLY WAS THE END OF THE WORLD.

I was squatting on the ground wanting to cry and scream and bawl but not being able to do any of them when a man walked into the veranda of the small house with the two rabbits on the wall; he came from within the dark interior of the house and stood there looking at me as if I was crazy; he wore a pair of shorts and a white gauze banian—sleeveless—and he was short and stocky with a square face and a thin mustache. Never taking my eyes off him I raised myself on my feet and took a few steps forward and trying to smile spoke a few words: "My rice ration books are lost."

He kept looking like he didn't know what I was talking about, and in that moment of silence I noticed he was a young man—young enough to be still going to school. Now a woman appeared on the veranda. I remember her now as being all gray—gray on the head, gray in the face and wearing a housecoat of gray material buttoned up in front from just below the neck right down to her ankles—for some strange reason this dress popular among urban lower-middle-class and working-class women was known as the "kimono" though it was a far cry from the Japanese kimono—and wore wooden sandals that made a sharp sound on the slate-colored rough cement floor. The young man—who must have been her son—said something to the woman and she looked at me suspiciously and then looked at Tony who was now by my side wagging his tail and trying to get friendly, and finally she looked hard at the gunny bag and the mirror placed against it. Slowly her gaze returned to me and she spoke in a thin reedlike voice:

"From where are you, boy?" In a long and uninterrupted sentence—for I didn't want to give her time to think—I rattled off my story and ended it with a polite request:

"Can I have some water to drink?"

She took some time to oblige and as she disappeared inside the house I noticed she was frighteningly thin and flat like a steamroller had gone over her, and then I heard the man's voice; Tony had attracted his attention at last.

"That's a good-looking dog," and Tony, who always understood when he was being referred to, was wagging the tail furiously.

I sat on the edge of the veranda on the floor—it was elevated slightly from ground level and I could sit and place my feet on the ground outside—and the man didn't invite me to sit on a chair. I was about to lean against the wooden pillar— one of the four that held the roof—when the woman appeared with a glass of water and I got up. The glass smelled vaguely of sardine and the water tasted like when it is taken from a galvanized bucket, but I drank it all in one breath and returned the glass to the woman with both hands, trying to look as grateful as I possibly could under the circumstances and immediately felt giddy and slightly out of breath and nauseous like when you want to throw up, and I sat down immediately on the edge of the veranda feeling awfully sick. I rested my back against the wooden pillar and felt something funny; I didn't feel the wood against my back because there was something inside my shirt. There was a moment of uncertainty—a split second when everything was suspended, a pause—and then a blinding explosion of sheer ecstasy. THE RATION BOOKS, THE RATION BOOKS WERE INSIDE MY SHIRT, AND I REMEMBERED THEN HOW I PUT THEM INSIDE MY SHIRT FOR SAFETY. I HAD PUT THEM IN FRONT BUT AS I WALKED THEY HAD QUIETLY SLIPPED TO MY BACK.

I sprang up and twisted and turned and bent trying to pull the books from behind my back, and the gray woman and her son with the square face were staring at me like I was the craziest thing they had encountered in their lives. The books were partially wet with sweat but still had the smell of fresh biscuits, and I was grinning from ear to ear and wanting to shout and scream with joy and not caring a hoot what the gray woman and her square-faced son thought, because I felt right on top of the world with not a pain anywhere in my body and the nausea had vanished and I wanted to run all the way home—to our new home beyond the Wijerama Junction on the gravel road that went by the army camp past the rubber trees—waving the new ration books that were safe and secure and smelled like fresh biscuits.

I sailed past Maharagama, the sleepy little new town, which looked like it had turned around abruptly to face the new road; Piyasoma Stores, which still faced the old road but had opened its back to the new road; the little yellow-colored bus with the legend ELMO RURAL BUS CO. painted on the sides and totally out of proportion to the body, which was really half a bus and looked like a halved loaf parked under the hik tree—Maharagama is still referred to as Hikgashandiya or the junction of the hik tree by the elders of the area; the shoe repair shop, with a crude reproduction of a John White shoe on its board—the dark-skinned man seated on a bench and mending a shoe I knew was Mr. Nugara because he would come visiting homes in Depanama to mend shoes on Sundays; and just beyond that facing the main road, the petrol shed with the Caltex star—all float past me like traveling shots in a movie, and then there's a slowing down of the pace, the images begin to hold longer—the Bo tree where the old road merges once again for a few hundred yards and then begins to run separately on the left hand side, and once more there are large and old houses set inside large gardens on either side—a stretch where one feels the continuity of life going back a long way into the past.

CUT.

Wattegedara. A mellow amber light falls from the western sky but when I look back towards the east from where I came the heavens are dark and foreboding and I think I hear the rumble of distant thunder. But everything is cool and relaxed, and the traffic on the road has increased. There are more carts than motor vehicles and the bulls amble along with the carters nodding under the awning, the ropes gone limp in their hands, and they are all moving eastwards towards where the sky is dark. But there is no hurry and everything moves to a leisurely rhythm. Near the Wattegedara Junction the feeling of antiquity persists in the narrow-story building with the trellis-worked balcony; the low-roofed row of boutiques with boarded fronts and shadowed by giant mara trees that would have slowly matured over more than a century. Here the High Level Road cuts through a ridge once again and ironically is on a lower level to the old road that runs over the ridge.

I felt like a cup of tea very badly, but the boutiques were full of people and I moved on, feeling very brave and very strong and very purposeful. My fingers hurt badly where they gripped the wooden edge of the mirror frame and the loops of the gunny bag—but that did not matter.

The High Level Road sloped gently down through the ridge and the old road came over the embankment on the left and the two roads met again just before another Bo tree—how come there are so many Bo trees along the old road especially where there was a junction of sorts? I wondered for a long time before I gathered much later in life that all those trees marked the spots where the legendary Buddhist revivalist Anagarika Dharmapala preached during his campaign and the British, sharp enough to observe that behind the Buddhist campaign was a national campaign which, in turn, was a political campaign, which again meant the British rule was threatened, countered by building a public lavatory wherever the Buddhists had planted a Bo tree, and true enough there were public lavatories near Bo trees at Borella, Pettah, and Kirulapona, but there were no such public conveniences near Bo trees along the High Level Road or the old road because there were enough open spaces in these parts then for people to relieve themselves—at which point the old road crossed on to the other side and moved away from the new road for good and just past the Bo tree on the old road was a road sign indicating a level crossing, which meant the rail track was close by.

I kept to the new road and passing the Bo tree on my right and a little temple with a small white dagoba down below on my left the road took a wide crescent-like bend just above a paddy field; the paddy was ripe and heavy with grain, and the field beginning like a corridor between the highland on the edge of which the road ran, and a thick woodland on the other side, broadened to a vast panorama of golden-brown in the distance; on the right of the road—to my right as I walked—the little railroad reappeared on a higher elevation following the same curve of the High Level Road, and here was the Nawinna Railway Station—a picturesque little building, more like a cottage in a picture postcard, and its walls were made of uncut granite washed over with white paint, and each block of granite was framed with a square molded in relief from the white plaster itself. From the edge of the roof paved with flat Calicut tiles hung little flower pots like at the Morawaka dispensary at Depanama. Behind the railway station was a strip of bare land with thick bushes, and above the bush rose a massive building, its white walls discolored to a dull gray and at first glance looking very much like an overcast sky because the walls were so high—the warehouses of the Colombo Commercial Company with the logo of the three overlapping C's embossed on the front wall over the huge iron roller-doors. No activity could be seen as the thick bush in the strip of land between the station and the warehouses rose high and the building looked silent, mysterious, and foreboding, like it held some dark secrets and belonged to some other world.

(Forty-five years later I killed myself trying to capture something of this atmosphere in the opening scene of *Pitagam-karayo*, and the paddy field on which the final sequence was staged was the very same paddy field that begins here—below the High Level Road below the rail track and facing the Naw-inna Railway Station—and stretching in an ever widening expanse around the village of Egodawatta, goes all the way beyond the Bellanwila Temple to end in the Attidiya marsh).

On the left hand side of the High Level Road, by the edge of the land that fell in a slope to the paddy field, were leafy mara trees again—much younger than the ones at Wattegedara and most probably as new as the new road, but their canopies had already spread in umbrellas of luxuriant green. The amber light was slowly receding over the field and far away where the golden-brown expanse took a right turn and disappeared, the sky was turning a deep red. The sound of distant thunder came from the east.

I stopped not because I was tired like when I stopped before, but because it looked the kind of place where one should stop. Tony was straining at the coir string and I knew he wanted to pee and he led me down the slope to the edge of the paddy field where the "pita-ela"—the outflow canal that runs on the edge of all paddy fields—flowed, and Tony didn't pee but went straight to the stream and started to drink—he certainly knew his way around paddy fields and knew exactly where the water flowed, like a cat smelling fish from a great distance. "Lap, lap, lap," drank Tony and the little fish broke formation and swarmed around his muzzle flashing gold and silver and I put my fingers in the water and the fish came rushing to peck and I felt warm and good like when I did that on the streams on the paddy field bordering the land where we lived after shifting from the big house. The water in the stream was warm from the sun and the smell of ripened paddy mixed with the smell of mud was like in Depanama when Anton and I went collecting fish in Horlicks bottles.

Tony was still lapping and my hands were still in the water with the fish pecking and the smell of paddy and mud all around me when I heard the whistle of the train and it was like someone calling. I clambered up the slope dragging Tony along just when the Little Train emerged from the bend coming from Colombo and going towards from where I came. The wagons rolled and the sound of iron wheels on iron rails was soothing to me. Thick clouds of smoke billowed from the funnel, hung in the air and began to scatter and then with that grinding sound that always gave me gooseflesh the train came to a halt and from where I stood I saw pure white steam swooshing from under the wheels of the black engine and somewhere within me I felt light and happy. Now the amber light was gone from the paddy field and I felt night approach from behind, from somewhere beyond that slope in the road that led back to where I came from but I felt no hurry to get going and I sat down under a mara tree leaning against the trunk and waited for the train to pull out of the Nawinna Station.

MIX.

Now I was walking the last few yards on the road before it reached the Nawinna hill, and passing a large house set deep inside a garden on an elevation enclosed by a brick wall with the name Llewelyn Senaratna written in white letters on the gatepost, I still couldn't see beyond the top of the hill because from where I was I couldn't see the drop on the other side.

A few minutes later I stood on the top of the hill and looked down into the sharp descent to a point where I could see once again the edges of a paddy field, and from that point I could see the road moving up again like a shiny black ribbon. At the end of that sharp rise there was a blur and after some time I could separate the tall slate-colored building from the gray of the road—and that building is, as you approach from Nawinna along the High Level Road, the first landmark you see of Wijerama Junction.

Land ahoy!

The train came straight at me and then went over as if I was in a pit under the wheels and it rumbled like thunder and there was a red light that glowed like a monstrous eye and became bigger and burst in a flash of white and everything became still and dark and silent; the train came again and the whole sequence repeated itself, over and over again like a looped movie . . . and I became larger and larger like a balloon being inflated; hands bloated like dead fish and I felt my head expanding, pressurized from within; through it all there was the sound of water dripping, rain falling on the tiled roof, rain leaking through and falling drip drip into something; rain rain go away come again another day and Rita was trying to get me to say it properly—it's not *jo* but *go* . . . say it . . . *go* and I wasn't getting the hard *g* sound and kept saying rain rain jo away and I was seated on Rita's lap and she smelled of Yardley's Lavender Talcum from the nice jar with the golden lid with a silver-colored label with a woman in a frilly dress . . . and then came the train again screaming hissing puffing with the red monster's eye and it rolled over me again and something exploded in a deep boom and now I was feeling cold and my legs were shivering knees knocking against each other and my hands between my legs curling and uncurling pressed against my thighs with clenched fists but the cold wouldn't go away and kept shaking me and cutting and stabbing me and it hurt badly with my teeth chattering and my head blooming and Father's voice droning sabbhantharaya-bhaya-dukka-pinang-makanthang-sabhithi-rogagraha-dhosa-masesa-ninda . . . and the red fish hanging over my head and the pink mosquito net all around me and through it the window and beyond that the coconut treetops because we were on the upper floor of the house and mother sponging me with a hot towel because Dr. Roy Dias was due any moment and the fresh smell of eau de cologne all over and the piece of cloth dipped in cologne cold and fine against my forehead and then the pink net was dissolving and the red fish was slowly disappearing but Father's voice keeps droning away . . . sabbhantharaya-bhaya-dukkha. . . .

First I heard the silence.

It was awful and scary in the beginning and it pressed down from all sides. Then I saw the window. It had a green frame with rusted iron bars across which sagged a curtain improvised from a piece of an old sari. It was the white voile sari with clusters of purple flowers Mother used to wear for months until it broke into little pillow covers for Sister when she was born and also a coverlet for the cot; now it has become a window curtain. The panes had opened outwards but I could see an edge of one of the panes where it caught the sun and that edge was green too—faded dirty old green. Beyond that was another green, leaves, wet and glistening in the sun, and looking unusually fresh and clean. Then slowly like a picture coming into focus, the sounds became clear, sharpened and tuned; the demalichchas were keeping up a chorus not very clear and it was vague in its shrill pitch and took time to separate from the atmosphere to become a sound; then I heard the crows, not all at once but intermittently and not in one place but from here and there far and near; the clang of a galvanized bucket on a cemented floor—it has to happen near a well with a cemented pavement encircling it and this sound must invariably be followed by another—the sound of the iron pulley as the rope bearing the bucket runs over it—and it came, the creaking grating metallic sound like iron wheels on rails and it always gave me gooseflesh. Then I thought I heard the whistle of the Little Train. It was so far away and so faint that I wondered whether I heard it at all; just then Mother came into the room.

Mother came with a cup in hand and along with her came the smell of Horlicks, the warm and familiar smell of after-fever-time. She kept the cup on Father's writing table—the small one, for the big one with four drawers on either side and baize-lined top along with the swivel chair (now I loved to swivel on that chair and felt bad to see it go) was sold to Proctor Gunawardane—and placed one hand on my forehead. I didn't know what she felt for she neither looked grave nor smiled but silently gave me the cup of Horlicks and went about tidying the room like she always did after I woke up and lay in bed in the mornings. Mrs. Mendis—now she and her family occupied one half of the house—theoretically that was, because in fact they occupied two thirds of the house and Mother felt we had been cheated in the affair—came silently from behind Mother and stood at the doorway. She said something to the effect of "Is the clever boy up?" kind of thing and Mother only turned half towards her and I had the feeling that something's not quite all right between them. I sat up in bed. It had been three days—I came to know later of course—since I had got into that position.

Three days before, when it was almost nightfall and Mother was practically dumb with fear I had walked in carrying the mirror, the gunny sack with milchard and Masoor dhal and brown sugar and "Amerikkan piti" and Tony tied to my waist buckle with a thin coir rope and I had walked in with a flourish, and looking cool as a cucumber had asked Mother for a glass of water. According to Mother, I had a grin on my face that frightened her, and according to Mrs. Mendis, she had quickly fetched a big glass of water that I had drained in one big breathless swallow, returned the glass to her, taken one step forward and fallen flat on my face. I couldn't remember any of that and I still can't. My final memory of that long march from Depanama was of my standing on the top of Nawinna hill and seeing the cement-colored building at Wijerama Junction. After the collapse on the doorstep I had lain for three days and three nights in a strictly horizontal position blazing with fever and talking gibberish in a delirium.

Now seated in bed and holding the cup of Horlicks in one hand, I looked down at Mother, who was picking up an aluminum bowl that had collected rainwater leaking through the roof the previous night, and very casually asked where Tony was. She straightened up without answering me and threw the water in the bowl out of the window — now it requires a certain skill to throw water out of a small window with bars where the lower half is covered with a curtain (that piece of a voile sari hung loosely over a string) and I was observing how Mother performed that feat making the water go clean through the narrow space between two bars — and now I glanced back at the doorway where Mrs. Mendis was standing when I looked down at mother to ask about Tony. Mrs. Mendis had vanished and now Mother walked out of the door and I heard her say that Tony is gone and her voice sounded like she was angry. I just sat there on the edge of that iron bed with its springs creaking whenever I made the slightest movement and began to drink the Horlicks.

Tony was certainly gone. I knew it from the moment I woke up and heard that terrible silence outside. Now I wanted to follow Mother to wherever she was going and I knew she would enter the hall from the veranda and crossing a little corridor would enter a long open back veranda at the end of which was the kitchen — and ask her why Tony was gone, when he was gone and where, but couldn't bring myself to doing it and just sat there drinking from the cup and not wanting to do anything.

The strangest thing was—and I remembered it as clearly as if it happened yesterday—that I wasn't feeling surprised or shocked or angry or anything like that. It was as if I had known this would happen all along. The story came in bits and pieces over the next few days. Each one knew some part of what had happened but there was something missing and I had the feeling they were holding it back not only from me but also from themselves.

According to Mother, when I had collapsed on the doorstep Sirisena's mother had jumped over the stile, came rushing and collecting me and cradling me in her arms like I was a baby had screamed for some lime and when that was brought had rubbed it all over my head and forehead chanting all the time and I had relaxed and even opened my eyes and smiled. Now Sirisena's mother had been among a few neighbors who had gathered at our doorstep on hearing the news of my having not returned till late in the afternoon when I should have returned by lunchtime. They had been with Mother for nearly an hour calming her and giving her courage and telling her that if I was ten years old I am big enough to find my way back home and Depanama was after all not so far away and there were many people at Egodawatta who had connections with Depanama and that Eliza who lived close by was a Gamage woman from Depanama and then mother realized this woman to be carter John's sister—and carter John was very well-known in Depanama being the man who rescued the British pilot who crash-landed in the paddy field at Polwatta during the Japanese air raid and took him to the dispensary in a hackery. Then I had appeared on the crest of the road just beyond the Lavanis boutique and the crowd in front of our house had watched in silence my progress for the next two or three minutes as I walked steadily and with that grin on my face that frightened my mother; once the initial surprise was over and Mother had to be restrained from pitching into me to release the tension within her, the crowd was dispersing when I collapsed and Mrs. Mendis had let forth a shrill scream, which is what brought Sirisena's mother running and jumping over the stile. Now this woman's son by whose name we identified her at the beginning was a dark lanky boy of about my age who lived with his mother and sister in a tiled house in the compound adjoining ours, and who wore a pair of navy blue shorts and nothing on top and befriended me the very next day after our arrival here and was a crack marble player who played me out of all my marbles on the first game we played.

Minutes after Sirisena's mother's mantram with the piece of lime had recovered me, the heavens had opened up. It had been the most furious thunderstorm in many years—and this is one point on which all their versions of the story are consistent— and it had lashed unabated throughout the night and well into high noon the next day, when there was a short break before it returned with greater fury by afternoon and roared boomed and crashed deep into the night.

Tony had found refuge under my bed—there were two beds in the small room kept adjacent to each other and against two walls—and Father came home in the night through the storm and drenched to his skin and wanted the dog out of the room. Mother could have resisted and had her way—she normally does when she feels strongly about something and Father usually gives in—but I suppose deep within her she also wanted Tony out of the room because with me on bed and blazing with fever (after Sirisena's mother's mantram made me open my eyes and smile I had gone into a deep sleep and within half an hour developed a very high temperature). Father had to be given the other bed, which meant Mother and Sister would have to sleep on the floor and it would be natural for any mother not to keep her two-year-old child next to a dog in the night. So she had coaxed Tony out from his lair and tied him up in that long open veranda at the back from where the poor animal, quite unaccustomed to such treatment, had kept up an unceasing spell of barking moaning and howling through the night. Now only a thin wall had separated the Mendis's bedroom from this back veranda and Mr. Mendis having returned after the late-shift—he was an English proofreader at the *Times of Ceylon*—was quite annoyed by this racket and a couple of times had opened the back door and—according to Mrs. Mendis— "only shouted at the dog to keep quiet"—but according to Mother had untied the dog and had kicked him—she was sure she heard the dog yelp—and Tony had come running through the pouring rain around the house and started scraping the door to our room while moaning and whining all the time and Father had got mad and beat him—"I hit him several times with the flat side of the foot ruler" insisted Father, meaning that this wouldn't have hurt him at all. But the moment Father closed the door the scraping and the whining and the moaning started all over again and now Mother came out and went around the house in the pouring rain and brought the chain and tied up the dog in the front of the house inside the veranda; now the veranda had only a half-wall enclosing it and the rain would have come inside, making it pretty uncomfortable for poor Tony but, according to Mother, he became quiet.

In the morning there was a big commotion: Tony had defecated in the veranda, and according to Mrs. Mendis it was the most unbearable stench she had ever experienced in her life, but according to Mother it was not that bad; certainly not as bad as when her two kids did the job—now the Mendises had two children, a girl of six named Shanthi and a four-year-old monster of a boy named Sarath who screamed around the clock asking for things to eat and drink. Mother had cleaned the veranda but Mrs. Mendis had kept washing the place over and over again and my little sister could not be brought out into the veranda because it was all wet and slippery. The rain continued and Mother had to go around the house to get to the kitchen because the Mendises had closed the main door into the hall, saying it was getting muddy. Once again Tony had been tied in the back veranda and according to Mother he was very quiet the whole day as if he realized the damage he had done.

But when night came and the doors were closed the barking started all over again. The storm had slowed down to a drizzle now, which made things more audible and, according to Mother, the dogs in the neighborhood would have heard Tony's bark for the first time, and they were reacting furiously. Soon the whole village had exploded into a tumult of barking. Then comes the gray area in the narrative. According to both Mother and Father, in about an hour's time the rain ceased altogether and there was absolute silence. The barking too had stopped. Father had gone around the house to check and found only the chain tied to the wooden post. Tony had gone. Mrs. Mendis distinctly remembered hearing Father go around the house to the back, but in her version Tony was still barking and all the dogs in the village were barking and the rain had not ceased at that time. Mother swears to say she heard Mr. and Mrs. Mendis muttering in the next room and then she heard a door latch open softly and within the next few minutes Tony stopped barking and one by one the dogs stopped barking and then the rain stopped and there was silence. It was then that she woke Father up and asked him to go check whether Tony was there.

The next morning when the doors opened Tony was gone and after three days the rain had stopped. That was the morning I woke up.

That evening Father came home early. After the rains everything was clear. Through the thick foliage surrounding our house the sky was blue, and towards evening daylight held a little longer. At six in the evening it was still not dark and I was seated on the edge of the veranda when Father appeared over the crest just beyond the boutique—which is exactly how Mother would have seen me appear that evening. Father came slowly with measured steps and head bent slightly forward as if he was carrying something on his back. When he saw me he appeared to look surprised at first and then he smiled like he was happy to see me. I stood up and he crossed the stile, jumping awkwardly over the bamboo poles and walking up placed a hand on my head, and then I knew he was not mad at me for doing what I had done.

Later, when night had fallen and lamps—little lamps with blackened and cracked chimneys—were lit, Father was talking to me; he was seated in the veranda and I was on a little stool; Mother was inside the room behind me and feeding Sister. Mr. Mendis was in the hall inside the house reading a paper but trying to catch Father's attention and somewhere in the kitchen Sarath—the monster—was screaming for more fish. Mr. Mendis had come earlier too and he was in a high state of excitement because Mr. S.W.R.D. Bandaranaike's driver and Sir John Kotalawela's driver had gone into fisticuffs near the Parliament and in the newspaper that Mr. Mendis brought there was a cartoon showing the two drivers—it was obvious they were the drivers because they were wearing checked sarongs and coats and had walrus moustaches and hair on the head spread and shaped like a traveler's palm—pummeling at each other and behind them two large shadows of Bandaranaike and Kotalawela engaged in a similar combat. Father however was more interested in talking to me. He had launched into one of those long talks he was fond of delivering to me whenever I was the source of some problem.

After the rains the frogs were croaking and I was listening to their sound and I heard Father's voice in the background; he was saying that what I did could have been a noble deed if not for one thing, which is that I had done it without consulting my elders; boys of my age should always consult their elders before doing such things, and they should always abide by what the elders say; now if I had done what I had done because either my mother or father had asked me to do it, then it would certainly be considered a noble deed. I wanted to tell Father that if I asked my elder's permission to do what I did I would never have been allowed to do what I did, and on the other hand if they asked me to do what I did I would never have done it, but I kept mum and listened to the frogs. I thought there were hundreds of them now drowning Father's voice and he was telling me for the millionth time about Casabianca, the boy who stood on the burning deck because his father asked him not to move from there under any circumstances and I thought as I always thought that Casabianca did a stupid thing by sticking there on that burning deck because when his father asked him to stay there he wasn't ever expecting the deck to catch fire; and now Father was moving on to his other favorite story of the six hundred horsemen who rode into the valley of death because "Their's not to reason why, their's but to do and die"— six years later my English teacher, Mr. Ariyaratne (may he attain nirvana) grinned sarcastically at a class of confused Senior form students and said that each one of those six hundred idiots richly deserved to die, and that according to him (Mr. Ariyaratne) both "Casabianca" and "The Charge of the Light Brigade," which had been dinned into our heads from childhood, were nothing but "supreme examples of British imperial stupidity," but that was in the future; now I was seated in our miserable little veranda still damp from the torrential downpour of the last three days and pretending to listen to Father telling me of six hundred British soldiers and their shining example of obedience, while I was really listening to the frogs who were multiplying every minute; now there were thousands of them croaking in a dizzying variety of pitches and tones, and through it all I heard Sarath the monster screaming hysterically in the kitchen. I very much wanted to tell Father that my idea in bringing Tony home was not because I wanted to do anything heroic like the boy who stood on the burning deck, or the six hundred horsemen who rode into the valley of death, or on the contrary not even because I wanted to do anything naughty and bad to annoy my parents—I had done such things in the past—but simply because I felt bad about leaving Tony behind after he had been with us for such a long time. I also wanted to tell Father that by the time I collapsed under those mara trees just after Roslin Nona's store and went to sleep I gave up hope of ever reaching home, but woke up and kept going because there was nothing else I could have done; I couldn't have gone back—gone back where? I couldn't have lain on the roadside either, because soon it would have been dark and there was a hint of rain in the air. I had no choice but to keep going until I dropped dead; now this had nothing to do with bravery or a sense of duty or obedience like in the case of poor Casabianca or those six hundred doomed horsemen. But I just kept silent and listened to the frogs whose sound was now becoming a deafening roar.

Mother, having put Sister to sleep, came out and stood in the doorway and said something to the effect that it would help her if Father finished his dinner now. Father stood up in response and, before proceeding into the little hall for his dinner, passed final judgment and closed the case; he said that Tony was a most ungrateful animal to have run away like that after I went through all that trouble to bring him home, and it is best that I forget the wretched dog.

That night I couldn't sleep because the frogs kept croaking. I felt as if there were millions of them now and they were not only croaking but braying, neighing, roaring and trumpeting. Father was peacefully snoring away on one bed and Mother was sleeping with Sister on the other—the one I occupied when I was running a high temperature for three days—and I was back on the floor where I kept tossing and turning, unable to sleep. A table lamp with a smoke-blackened chimney was burning low and in its dim light I saw Mother turning in bed towards me. She knew I was awake and spoke to me in a low but clear voice—her voice was always low but very clear and sharp and she spoke slowly enunciating each word very carefully. She said to me that night that I shouldn't worry about Tony, that he would certainly have gone back to Depanama where he would be all right because there were people there who knew him and liked him and would look after him. It is better it happened this way, because here Tony would have been very unhappy. Now you go to sleep.

Listening to her I felt good in a long time, and one by one the frogs stopped croaking and everything became still and silent, and I fell asleep.

In the days that followed, the sun was bright, and slowly the air turned hot and the pools of water in the bare fields evaporated leaving the ground soft and muddy, and the koha began to cry. I was busy losing my marbles to Sirisena and though I had collected them lovingly over five years, now I was not sad to lose them because it was the marbles that qualified me to join Sirisena and his gang; yes there was a gang and all of them bare-bodied except Munidasa who always wore a banian when he came to play and he wore socks and shoes to school and carried his books in a small brown-colored suitcase, which meant he went to an English medium school; there was another fat boy whose name I mistook to be Ronald because the others called him "Ranal" and I thought that was a mispronunciation of Ronald, but everyone laughed when I called him Ronald and I went along with the others and called him Ranal—the first *a* as in "rat" and the second syllable as the "nel" in tunnel—and I still haven't quite traced the origins of that name; there was another fellow quite big for his age and with a large head whose name was Ratnapala, but everyone called him "Theliya," which was the name of a large fish with an ugly snout like a bulldog's and found in the village streams, and I was told that "Theliya" the boy was very fond of catching fish and someone told him it is very easy to catch fish in the night because they go to sleep, and he (Theliya) slipped out of his home in the middle of the night and got lost in the vast paddy fields in the dark and there was pandemonium in the village when his mother started screaming as if someone was dead and Theliya was found in the middle of the field shaking and shivering like he had seen a ghost and he couldn't talk until there was a devil dance to chase away the demon who had possessed him.

Each afternoon when the boys returned home from school they would come and stand silently by the bamboo stile leading to our house, and I would dip into that black jar that held those marbles for me for well over five years, and take a handful of shining sparkling glass balls and join them and Mother wouldn't stop me—Mother who would never let me play with the village children at Depanama had now suddenly become indifferent to my activities—and I didn't know whether it was because she was too tired or I was getting too big for her or she let me go because that way I would forget Tony.

The game of marbles would begin right in front of our house on the gravel road and proceed ball by ball, throw by throw, and shot by shot, along the meandering path between fences lined with rubber trees and albizzia bushes all the way down to the paddy field. By the time we reached the paddy field my marbles would be gone but daylight was still bright on the brown haystacks that stood like giant anthills all over and the sun was hanging like a big ball of fire at the far end beyond the Kesbewa road and beyond the Bellanwila Temple.

One day we moved in the other direction, the direction from which I walked with Mother into Egodawatta for the first time and from where I would have come bringing Tony in the late evening—and we moved playing on the edge of the road past the Lavanis boutique and a little cluster of houses surrounding it, and then by the edge of the rubber plot—dark and mysterious in the corridors under the trees—and then down the slope where on the left was a big house with a tiled roof and a long open veranda resting on thick columns—the veranda was almost empty like in an abandoned house but for an easy chair with a broken bottom and a framed scroll hanging above the doorway and the house had not been whitewashed in years and looked like it was about to collapse—and I was told this was where Ranal lived, and there appeared on that empty veranda a fair and buxom woman with her hair tied in a top knot and wearing a bodice, which barely covered her ample breasts, and a faded chintz cloth hitched up, revealing one varicose-veined leg up to the knee—and she, I was told, was Ranal's mother, and I was also told that Ranal had no father.

The woman paused in the doorway that led from the veranda to the interior of the house and Ranal stopped on the road and Sirisena who swung his arm backwards to shoot his marble stopped in midaction and then as if by some secret and silent communication we all stopped wherever we were on the road. The woman—Ranal's mother—took a few steps forward and stood on the edge of the veranda and in a high-pitched voice—which didn't seem to be coming from her but from somewhere else—said something a word of which I couldn't understand because all the syllables merged into each other in an unbroken series of sounds, but obviously Ranal understood because he lowered his head and began walking up the three cemented steps that led from the road to the front compound and he was taking one step at a time like he was reluctant to go, and his mother stood on the edge of the veranda looking quite angry.

The boys were turning their heads one by one in the opposite direction and when I turned I saw first a Burgher gentleman wearing khaki shorts and a boxing banian cleaning a gun and then behind him a house with steps leading to it on two sides, and on the side directly facing the road a girl was seated. The Burgher gentleman threw a bored glance at us and was about to concentrate on his gun when as if on second thought he looked up again and kept looking at me, his eyes getting smaller and smaller, and then referred to my father by name and asked me in English whether I was the son and when I said yes he lowered his gun and walked up to the edge of the steps leading down to the road—here too there was a flight of three short cemented steps leading up to the garden from the road, because at this point the narrow gravel road cut through the undulating land on an even level—and began talking with me in English and immediately Sirisena and the boys withdrew a few steps from me like they were feeling uncomfortable, I couldn't quite listen to what the Burgher gentleman was saying because I was distracted by the girl on the steps who kept her legs parted and turned up at the knees and I could see right through to the white knickers she was wearing and I noticed the boys were getting pretty restless too; they kept shifting on their feet and kicking the ground and trying desperately to look away but their eyes kept coming back to the girl and they were pretending not to see what they saw — milky white legs right up to the thighs and beyond to a flash of white knickers, and the girl kept doing whatever she was doing—I don't remember what she was doing because that was totally eclipsed by those unusually white legs—and she did not look up even once.

A woman's voice called from within the house and it called a name quite strange to me at that time—Cleone! Yes, that was the name called and the girl stood up and never once taking her eyes from whatever she was doing, turned around and walked inside the house. Though she never looked up at us, there was something about the way she walked that made me feel she was quite aware of us and our eyes on her. With those white legs gone I felt immediate relief for I was worried sick that the Burgher gentleman would catch me looking at the girl and I couldn't stop looking either. But by now the danger was past and Mr. Manger—yes, that's who he told me he was and wanted me to tell my father that I met and spoke with him—had gone back to cleaning his gun. Sirisena and the gang had started moving down the road and I joined them, but now they were not talking, not even looking at each other and moving silently like they were guilty of something. Each one knew that the others had seen him looking at those white legs and that made each one feel very uncomfortable as if he was caught doing something dirty. I felt uncomfortable too, and wished like hell that Sirisena would start playing marbles again, but he kept throwing two marbles up in the air alternately and catching them expertly like a juggler, and I had three balls left with me, which I kept playing by myself along the ground, hoping to entice Sirisena or any other to resume playing, but each one was doing his own thing: kicking the ground, picking stones and throwing them aimlessly, and generally trying to avoid one another, and Theliya was whistling furiously, emitting only puffs and squeaks.

The road moved like a giant drain between the two compounds—Ranal's and Mr. Manger's—and where Ranal's compound ended, the RAF camp site began and from that point onwards on that side there was a barbed wire fence held together by those concrete columns with the top ends tilting outwards and inside was a smooth gravel drive running along the fence that turned and came back in a loop and in the middle of that loop was a well-laid-out garden with neatly clipped bushes and flowing creepers climbing over archways of steel pipes with wire mesh draped over them and facing this garden on the other side of the drive were two billets made of planed wood overpainted with green set at right angles to each other and on the two open verandas with rolled-up tats hanging in front were white-painted rattan chairs, and along the verandas that ran into each other at one end so that one could walk on them from one billet to another there hung beautiful lampshades at regular intervals. At the corner where Ranal's compound ended and the camp began, there was a brick building with walls unplastered but washed over with white so that the bricks showed, and on the wall was written in large black letters KITCHEN NO. 1 and as we came up to this point along the road I had the delicious smell of roast beef—I could immediately identify this smell for it was there every evening in and around Greenlands, Father's ancestral home at Havelock Town where he took me once-in-a-way to spend a few days and on either side of which were houses where white folks lived.

On the pavement just outside Kitchen No. 1 a man was seated on a wooden box, and he was pitch black and he had his crinkly hair spread from ear to ear in that travelers palm hairdo and he was wearing a spotlessly white apron, which made him look darker, and immediately on seeing him Sirisena and the boys broke their silence and, clinging on to the barbed-wire fence, began clamoring for ice. The boys addressed the dark man as "Number Wun Aiya" and he kept looking at them with drooping eyelids like he was half asleep and he was absolutely motionless; then the smokeless stump of a cigar moved slowly from one end of his thick-lipped mouth to the other and a gravelly voice drawled an order; in a moment a thin man emerged from the kitchen carrying a bowl of ice cubes, which he distributed among grabbing pushing shoving hands stretched out through the barbed wire. Now it was my turn to be aloof, and I watched the goings-on from the other side of the road. The boys were screaming and shrieking hysterically as they rubbed or pressed ice cubes on each other and they were jumping like being stung by bees. No one tried it on Sirisena and he walked calmly across the road to offer me some ice, which I refused—ice made me feel sick because the only time I had seen ice was when I had high fever and I used to watch in a delirium steaming blocks of it being shoved into the ice cap that was then placed on my burning head and I could hear the clink as they struck against each other when Mother moved the red-colored rubber pack around.

The screaming and the jumping was subsiding and the boys moved, sucking ice cubes and throwing them from hand to hand, to a patch of bare land facing the camp and that was on a higher elevation to the road. There we sat on a thick carpet of buffalo grass and behind us were sickly coconut trees with a dense undergrowth of bush around them and high above the even chorus of birdsong a lone squirrel kept up a frantic alarm call, and a huge truck with a dark-blue body and an eagle with its wings spread painted in yellow on the front door appeared on the drive within the camp. It moved like a great big animal almost silently, its engine making only a low humming sound, and it stopped where the road came back in a loop; the door with the eagle swung open and a white officer in a uniform of steel blue jumped out and closed the door hard. The truck pulled away towards Kitchen No. 1 and the white officer leapt from the driveway into the veranda of his billet and disappeared inside. The truck came back along the loop and moved towards where it came from and as it disappeared among the trees the notes of a piano came floating from inside the billet where the white officer went; the music was vaguely familiar and the smell of roast beef was still in the air coming from Kitchen No. 1 and I thought of the lonely nights I spent at Greenlands in Havelock Town, where I slept on a bed in the huge dining room with all those portraits of my ancestors looking down on me from the high walls reaching all the way to the dark intricately carved wooden ceiling, and the smell of roast beef hung in the air and I would always hear the notes of a piano floating in from somewhere, playing strange and sad yet beautiful melodies and I would miss the warmth of my mother and cry silently into the crisp white bed sheets and pillow cases, which were cold and smelled of starch and camphor.

Each year during the April season a giant wheel would be constructed in Depanama and it would be there till after Wesak; this year they were constructing it on the little hill overlooking the Pannipitiya Railway Station where once-upon-a-time there was a tennis court and every Saturday Father would come in the evenings to play tennis with Messrs. Arthur Kothalawala, Bulner, Subasinghe and the Station Master, Mr. Samarasinghe, and I would sit perched on the embankment by the cactus bushes with Guneris the servant boy and watch the trains come and go in the station down below, and during the Sri Pada season, which was from early January to late May, the trains were full of pilgrims and white cloth fluttered like birds' feathers from the windows, sheaths of areca nut pods bristled, voices chanted and along with them the iron wheels of the train braked, clanged and screeched, all blending together in perfect harmony and held together by the sad melancholy whistle of the train as it reached and left the station and behind was the sound of the tennis ball hitting the racquet the ground or the net in a soft but clear and varying rhythm, thuk, thik, thok, thook. Then one by one they stopped playing; Mr. Subasinghe disappeared because—I heard Mother and Father whispering to each other—his wife had run away with a Tamil gentleman who was the apothecary at the local government dispensary; Mr. Kothalawala had a stroke and was ordered complete rest; the Station Master, Mr. Samarasinghe, started drinking during the day also and was too drunk by evening to play tennis, and old Mr. Bulner simply stopped playing. We moved from the big house to the small one at Depanama and Father had no time to play for he left home early in the morning on a bicycle and would return late at night even on Saturdays, and sometimes he would be gone for days. And the tennis court was abandoned and weeds grew all over it and the iron roller used to level the court was dragged by some village boys to the top of the little hill and rolled down where it ended in a ditch and lay there like a broken animal.

Now the old tennis court had been cleared of weeds and a large crowd had gathered to watch the setting up of the giant wheel there, and it was the first week of April and exactly one month after we left Depanama and three weeks after I walked with Tony to our new home in Egodawatta and I was being sent back by Mother to return some money she had borrowed from Mrs. Lawrence Perera; the money was put in an envelope and stitched into my shirt pocket and in it was a note to Mrs. Lawrence Perera with a kind request to see that I don't end up doing something stupid like last time and this was in addition to Mother telling me firmly not to try anything fancy, and if I do, Father is going to be very angry not only with me but with Mother too, because Father doesn't know that I was being sent again to Depanama all alone etc., etc. . . . All this was quite unnecessary, for by now I had struck firm roots at Egodawatta and I was going to finish up with whatever I had to do at Depanama and be back as soon as possible, for Sirisena and the boys had planned a game of cricket in the paddy fields, which by now had become dry and hard, and they were going to wait for me. But I had a problem that kept bothering me. What if I were to meet Tony again at Depanama? If he had gone back there, he was sure to get my scent—he would start barking and whining a good five minutes before we could see the faint light of Father's bicycle appear in the dark at the far end of the gravel path that led to our small house at Depanama—and seek me out wherever I was around Depanama, and if that happened I couldn't quite figure out what I was going to do. The situation made me nervous in advance and I was quite tense as I walked from the bus stop past the old gateposts and along the macadam road winding above the railway station, and this was when I saw the crowd gathered near the old tennis court and saw the curve of the giant wheel against the hard blue April sky. The school holidays were on and there was a large number of schoolchildren and among them I saw Piyasena, Jayasena, and Jinadasa—three brothers who lived in a wattle-and-daub house on the edge of the paddy field within sight of the house we lived in, and who would come every evening and play with me in our backyard because Mother wouldn't let me go out and play with them—and they saw me and broke away from the crowd and came running up to me and, grinning from ear to ear, kept looking at me from head to foot like I had come from the moon, but I was in a mighty hurry and, mumbling some excuse, went on my way.

As I passed Ambagashatara and reached that stretch bordering Mrs. Jayasinghe's land my heart began to beat faster; this was the danger zone where any moment from anywhere Tony could burst forth like he did the last time and I was jumping and starting at every twig-breaking and leaf-rustling. The drums were beating at the Devale—each year after the harvest in April there was an all-night ritual of thanksgiving to the gods and for one week before that the drums would start beating—and the low mysterious tone of the devil drum always gave me a creepy feeling. Today it depressed me and I wanted to take the short cut through Mrs. Jayasinghe's land to get away from the sound of drums quickly and the sound came over the open land that sloped down to the paddy fields on the right of the road. But the short-cut through Mrs. Jayasinghe's land could become lonesome and scary at a certain point where it was gloomy under a massive tamarind tree and a little beyond that began Kendahena Estate—a rubber plantation where it was rumored a woman tapper was stabbed to death with a tapping knife and her ghost walks at noontime. So I kept to the normal route and reached Mrs. Lawrence Perera's house safely. Anton and his two sisters—Girlie and Freeda—had gone to Nuwara Eliya for the holidays—and I was happy for that because I could get away soon, but Mrs. Lawrence Perera insisted that I should have some lunch and I had to stay because she said Mother would blame her if I fell sick again like last time. I wanted to avoid talking about Tony but she brought the matter up and told me that Tony is here all right and I shouldn't worry about him because he has got used to Proctor Gunawardane's place where they give him food to eat and she saw him a couple of times and he looked all right.

I set off immediately after lunch and once more my heart started pounding because at a particular point in the gravel road along which I had to walk to reach the macadam road I could see across another compound to the rear of Proctor Gunawardane's house and I looked down and walked briskly and I was sick with tension. I had cleared the little climb just before the path joined the main road and was feeling relieved, when it happened. First I heard a faint whining sound and I closed my eyes immediately, and then there was the sound of rushing dog's feet and something fell heavily against my legs.

I opened my eyes and there at my feet lay Tony with upturned paws in that gesture of canine loyalty and affection. It was Tony and also not Tony. The dog who lay at my feet wriggling and moaning in a trance of affection was not the Tony I knew, not the dog with that beautiful coat who always smelled good and clean; this was a sick dog with sores all over; tufts of fur stood among patches of red skin through which the bones showed. I squatted by his side and stroked his head; only the face remained the same as ever, the fluffy ears, the cream-colored head with a light-brown shadow over the perfectly sculptured muzzle, and the same soft and gentle eyes that now kept looking at me eagerly and expectantly in pools of bubbling love.

I stood up and began walking slowly and Tony followed me. I paused briefly at the top of the gravel path where it joined the macadam road and Tony kept close to me. Across the road was the wattle-and-daub hut with the thatched roof where Mary Akka had her little hopper boutique. From where I stood I could see the glass case where the bread was kept. I crossed the road with Tony following me and he stayed on the road when I entered the boutique. There was no one to be seen and I tapped on the table on which the glass case stood. Mary Akka came from inside and when she saw me her face darkened. She seemed annoyed over something and went about silently opening the glass case and taking the bun out for me and wrapping it in a piece of paper; when I said the bun is for the dog she unwrapped it and, giving me the bun, shoved the piece of paper in a tin kept for that purpose. A bun was five cents and I gave her a twenty-five-cent coin and she took time bringing me the change. As I turned to go Mary Akka broke her silence. She wanted me to tell Mother that it was very bad on her part to have gone away without as much as a word of farewell; she also said that she wasn't thinking of the money we owed her. I had nothing to say and I walked out on to the road where Tony was waiting for me. He saw the bun in my hand and stood up on his hind legs sniffing eagerly, but I walked a few yards and he followed me, eyes fixed on the bun. When I gave him the bun—I gave it to his mouth—he held it lightly for a moment, undecided, then circled couple of times and still holding the bun in his mouth looked up at me. I squatted down on my haunches and then Tony settled down on all four legs and, keeping the bun between his paws like a squirrel would do, began eating slowly and rather indifferently; Tony always ate slowly even when he was hungry.

First I stood up, and Tony paused briefly in his eating, but when I stood still he went back to his bun, and then I took one step back, away from him, and he didn't notice, and another step, and then another, and another and Tony kept eating his bun. Then I turned around, closed my eyes and ran. I ran with the harsh midday sun burning all around me, past the Ambagashatara Junction, past Manchi Akka's boutique and never once looked back, and by the time I reached the spot where they were putting up the giant wheel overlooking the railway station I felt like my chest was going to explode—the crowd at the giant wheel site in the morning was gone and only a few people remained and they were resting on the ground taking a midday break, and the seats were now fixed on the wheel and it stood against the blinding glare of high noon turning slowly in the wind—and without running along the road I slipped through the cactus bushes, down the steep embankment, across the railway lines, and clambered on to the platform, which was a good four feet above the rails. My legs were wobbly and my head swam as I stood on the platform and looked up at the road above the embankment and beyond the row of cactus bushes. First it was a blur but slowly things came into focus and there was no dog on the road. Still panting I walked slowly along the platform and got back on the road where it crossed the railway line. I went through the old gateposts and reached the bus stop on the High Level Road. The bus was a long time in coming and I heard two trains come and go at the railway station. When finally the bus came after what seemed like a long long time, I knew the crisis was over.

I took a ticket to Wattegedara, which was a long way before Wijerama and just after Maharagama, for I had specific instructions from Sirisena how to reach Egodawatta through a short-cut, which was by a gravel road to the left of Wattegedara; by taking this path I would reach a paddy field within a max-imum of seven minutes, which was much less than what it would take me to walk from Wijerama to Egodawatta, and this paddy field at the end of the road from Wattegedara was the same one which stretched behind Egodawatta and where we would play hora polis in the evenings, and today Sirisena and the boys would be there waiting for me; we were going to play cricket and if we could finish the game before dark, the boys were going to show me the Boralesgamuwa Tank, and that was going to be the first time I would see a tank.

As the bus pulled away I looked at the High Level Road glistening like silver in the noonday heat and there was no dog on the road, and I knew that I would never see Tony again, and it would be a long long time before I revisited Depanama because there was nothing for me there anymore.

The Little Train

The Colombo-bound train from Avissawella would reach Udahamulla by seven thirty in the morning and I would leave home at Egodawatta one hour earlier when there were pools of darkness still under the trees, and it would take me a little more than thirty minutes to get to the station that stood on the edge of a paddy field beyond the public cemetery and you walked between old tombstones and descended a slope to the old road that lay behind the station; now there was no station at Udahamulla like the one in Pannipitiya; there was no solid brick building but a wood cabin with just enough room for the booking clerk—yes there was no Station Master either—to sit and issue tickets, receive and send signals, and perform many other duties and the place was called a halt, but from around five thirty in the morning when the first trains started running a large crowd would be there till nine, and the platform was broad and long enough to accommodate the crowd and was quite out of proportion to the little cabin that stood like a dog house in the middle. School was at Nugegoda and, that being the next stop on the railroad towards Colombo, the train reached there a few minutes to seven thirty, and I had plenty of time to amble along Church Street with its neat little cottages set high on the slope on the left and reached by flights of steps lined with potted plants and flaming bougainvillea creepers. From mid December right through the first months of the following year a mist rolled down from the hill above the roof tops and hung over the street in the mornings and then it would be cold and chilly and dark in the shadows and I would think of Nuwara Eliya where I had been once with Mr. Lawrence

Perera and his family because Anton had insisted that I be taken because I was his best friend and when I thought of Anton I thought of Depanama and then memories would come one after the other and then I heard a barking—it was Tony barking and the flow of memories would stop abruptly at that point like the image-freeze in a movie, but the barking would continue; Tony's image was blurred and faded like an old snapshot, but I heard the bark, sharp and clear, whenever there was a mist over Church Street and I heard it high above the sad whistle of the Little Train as it was leaving the Nugegoda Station and crossing the road behind me and I walked slowly up the street and through the mist and the cold, and the Burgher girls in their immaculate white uniforms came floating down like angels from the cottages along the slope and stepped daintily into the black asphalt of the street.

At Egodawatta we had moved house once again—moved from the half-a-house to a full one just a few hundred yards closer to the paddy fields; it was a very old house with a sloping roof lined in front by a valance board of intricate design like a piece of embroidery and held together on either side by two gabled walls—unplastered on the outside and showing red brick masonry, giving the impression of an unfinished construction. There was a large veranda resting on three masonry columns, open in front and walled on either side and on each wall was an arched opening divided in the middle by a bar and the entire house reminded me of Geera Atha's place in Depanama—the old house with the two framed rabbits—because the architecture was identical, and this house at Egodawatta, we were told, was where Sirisena's mother—the lady who chanted mantram when I collapsed after walking home with Tony—was born, and which meant it would have been half-a-century old, but there were old coffee plants all over the garden and they looked like the remains of a larger plot, which made Father pronounce that the house must have been built during the "Coffee Days" thereby implying it to be well over a hundred years old. The house now faced a plot of rubber where each morning Sirisena's mother tapped the trees, and during the fall when the trees were bare of leaves we could see the paddy field—the same field which began below the High Level Road in front of the Nawinna Railway Station, and where Tony dragged me to drink water from the "pitaela" and the sound of the Little Train came floating all the time—far away, but quite sharp and clear.

It was my second January since I began school and very nearly three years since we came to Egodawatta, and I was on my way to the Udahamulla Halt early in the morning.

I walked alone, for no other children from Egodawatta went to school that way; Sirisena went across the paddy field to Maharagama; Munidasa too went through the paddy field but he went the other way towards Boralesgamuwa and he left earlier because his school was at Dehiwela and he was accompanied by his father who worked at the Railway Workshop at Ratmalana; Theliya had gone away to his uncle's place at Grandpass and we were told he was attending a Colombo School; Ranal had dropped out of school and was working at his big brother's garage at Puttalam: "Ranal Yahampath, Club Garage, Colombo Road, Puttalam" was the address he gave me just before he left a year ago in 1951, which was a year after we came to Egodawatta and by which time Ranal and I had become good friends and he considered me his best friend because unlike the others I didn't tease him for not having a father and he would take me home and his mother liked me and always gave me sweets and said I looked like a respectable kid and the other boys in the gang told me their parents had asked them not to go to that house because Ranal's mother was a bad woman who was friendly with the white soldiers in the RAF camp.

The red earth on the road was wet with the overnight dew as I walked the hill and came to the shoulder bend on the road to Wijerama Junction and in front of me a thick mist lay over the empty ground, which rose up to where the RAF radio station stood, and a red light glowed through the gloom on the crest of the signal tower and the building was still a silhouette against the slowly brightening sky. I turned right and went briskly past the giant etamba trees on the left of the road because it was cold under the shade and a little beyond on the right of the road was another part of the camp where the billets were made of thatched coconut palms framed with slats and these were the quarters for "locals" and they were a mixture of Sinhalese, Tamils, Burghers, and Malays, and the sergeant was Mr. Dole who had his office and quarters in the only building there with a tiled roof and plastered brick walls. I walked on that side of the road by the barbed wire fence that separated the camp and the lights were still burning in the "huts" and the windows were propped open upwards on wooden hinges and I could see the soldiers getting dressed for the morning muster and I stopped at a particular point where I could see between the huts to the thick bush behind the camp and beyond that to the eastern sky. I looked up almost by instinct and slowly the shape of Sri Pada came into focus, barely visible at first, but my eye scanned the vague line and brought into relief the cloud-like mountain range in a darker shade of blue against a pale blue sky and now I was standing by the bay window on the upper level of the big house at Depanama and down below someone was drawing water from the deep well because the pulley was making that harsh grating sound of iron against iron and Mother was in the quadrangle wearing that wraparound kimono with a dragon on the back and over and above the trees I could see the paddy fields and beyond that I was trying to trace on the faraway sky the vague line of the blue mountains and Tony the mischievous pup was pulling at the fold of my pajamas demanding to be carried and the sad whistle of the Little Train began somewhere and kept coming closer and closer and then the train came, not charging and thundering, but gently like a float, its windows fluttering in white cloth-ends and shawls and bristling with white pods and as it reached the platform, voices rose up in chorus: "Sadhu, Sadhu," and wheels grated harshly on rails and the compartments collided with each other and the voices continued, now singing "Thun Sarane," and right throughout, behind me, the ball kept hitting the racquet or the ground or the net in a monotonous never changing rhythm, thuk, thuk, thik, thok, thook and then midway through the gorge before the Nugegoda Station the green signal was on and the train whistled in a long held note as it emerged between the two embankments, and looking out of the train window I could see the mist thick over the town and I was sure I would hear that bark as I walked up Church Street.

The turnaround bus scheduled to leave Wijerama Junction at seven thirty in the morning was already parked under the jak tree in front of Sunil Stores and most of the crowd going towards Colombo were seated inside but there were a few others waiting out by the roadside hoping to catch an earlier bus coming from Homagama or Maharagama, and I was on the other side of the road waiting for a bus going the other way because now I was going to school in the opposite direction to Nugegoda and each morning I would board the bus from Wijerama and proceed past Nawinna, Wattegedara, Maharagama, and all the way on the High Level Road to a point one bus stop beyond where once-upon-a-time Mother and I took the bus to Wijerama, leaving Tony behind. Six years had gone by and now it was the year 1956 as I waited for the bus—the only one waiting on that side of the road for a bus—to take me to school at Pannipitiya on a cold November morning. For three years now I had been traveling that way and back and all this time I had very carefully avoided any contact with Depanama, which lay on the other side of the High Level Road, but each morning and afternoon I was on the same route I had taken with Tony six years ago and I would love to take a corner seat and watch the road go by and recall each moment of that journey and each point on that road came to be associated with some stage of that walk and slowly it had become a secret addiction, something I wished to keep to myself, and boarding the bus each morning and afternoon was like the moment when you go to sleep and wait for the lights to go off so that you could retreat into your private world of fantasy and it becomes something you look forward to, and though at school I was quite active and outgoing, in the bus I hated company and became a different person and withdrew into myself.

The Homagama-bound bus came before the turnaround bus left Wijerama and it was practically empty as it always was in the morning—at that time of day life moved mainly towards Colombo—and soon I was on my way, down the slope from Wijerama and up again to Nawinna and the bus was moving very fast and it didn't stop at the Nawinna hill and began negotiating the corner and I knew the paddy field will soon come into view just round the bend and then I heard the train whistling far away and the bus took the turn and the railway station came into view and the train was reaching the platform and I saw it all through a thin haze, which was part mist and part smoke and steam, and then I looked towards the paddy field on the other side and the bus was just passing the spot where Tony and I went down the embankment to the field and Tony drank water from the "pitaela" and the fish swam around his muzzle and the paddy was ripe and heavy with grain and the smell of ripe paddy and mud was just like when Anton and

I went fishing in the fields at Depanama and now I am walking under the rubber trees with Tony and the ground is thick with dead leaves and my feet sink and spring like I am walking on a carpet and the air is damp and heavy with the smell of latex and from the trees I pull panel scrap—thin strips of rubber formed by dried residual latex along the tapping cuts to mesh together into a cricket ball—they were hard like leather balls and had a terrific bounce and could hurt real bad; Tony sniffs around and inspects each tree with great seriousness peeing all the time, and now I collect pod shells—ear-shaped and hard with a sharp edge like a thorn at one end on each side— and I hold the ends between my thumb and forefinger and blow hard into them and the shells spin with a low humming sound and the birds in the trees get agitated setting up alarms all over, screeching screaming and twittering and then the squirrels take over and soon there is a wild cacophony. (In the fall, which begins in November and lasts through February, rubber pods crack and burst, spilling seeds which have a brittle and brown outer shell and look like some birds' eggs, and the pod shells fall too and lie scattered among the dead leaves until the rains come in March—afternoon thunder showers as we were taught in school—to wash them away and make the ground clean and ready for new grass to grow, and the bare trees send forth pale-purple leaves, which in due time turn a tender green).

Tony is barking furiously at a garden lizard who has clambered on to high ground from the strip of marsh between the paddy field and the rubber land; the evil-looking creature twice the size of Tony is blowing and hissing like an angry dragon, scales bristling and the sharply edged swordlike tail swishing every now and then, and I get up and, taking a few steps back towards safer ground, throw a stone that bounces off the creature's scaly back and falls with a plop into the marsh beyond and a flock of white herons rise up in the air to flap flap flap gracefully in a circle and descend again among the tall green reeds, and "their breasts assuaged with sandal-paste and pearls, casting dark beams from wide eyes this way and that; the lovely Naga maidens couchon the clean sands..." Mr. Jayakody's voice is pitched somewhere between speech and song as he recites from the *Selalihini Sandeshaya* but I keep gazing at the nape of Padmini's neck, slender and graceful, with wisps of hair just above the collar of her white uniform where the pigtail begins, and "on the tips of their breasts the shining domba buds are wound like strings of pearls," continues Mr. Jayakody's monotone and I with a foot ruler gently lift the black-ribboned end of Padmini's pigtail and Karunatilaka on my right passes me the pencil—it's a delicate operation and has to be done with great patience, precision, and concentration—and "their eyes blue nymphaea, white lilies their smiles, their lips the red water lily, lotus-faced they seem" and I drop the end of the pigtail into the little slot on my desk—we used fountain pens but our desks coming from the late thirties still had slots to keep the ink pots steady—and now I look straight at Mr. Jayakody like I am spellbound while my hands work deftly under the desk, fixing the pencil cross-wise like a latch on Padmini's pigtail; "The sun's disc seems a ripened fruit, dark red, that nears the time of severance from its stalk," Mr. Jayakody recites and I withdraw my hands and place them clearly and firmly on the desk, clean well-behaved hands; the message has gone from desk to desk and now moments pass in nerve-racking silence; "Of that vast tree the sky, lovely as sapphire, blue on blue, washed by the evening winds that play about its region boughs" and pauses here Mr. Jayakody, the thick stubby hands holding the book are lowered, one hand goes up to push the horn-rimmed glasses on to the forehead and with a combined movement of the lips and tongue the dentures are adjusted; "What were the Naga maidens doing?" and up go half a dozen hands but both mine are placed neatly on the desk and I keep looking at Mr. Jayakody with a calm and serene expression, and then in a delayed reaction Padmini puts up her hand and Karunatilaka begins chewing on his fingernails desperately. Mr. Jayakody's eyes, small and deep within the sockets, move lazily across the class, go past Padmini and then come back to her; "Yes, you?" and Karunatilaka lowers his head and shuts his eyes. Padmini gets up, or half gets up and her pigtail is caught firmly in the slot on my desk and her head jerks back violently; she loses her balance shrieks like someone has squeezed her neck and falls sideways on the girl next to her and that girl screams in turn and now the entire class explodes in hysterical laughter; the pencil has snapped and Padmini is free but now the uproar is maintained deliberately; having broken through classroom order there is no wish to get back to it and in the confusion I see Mr. Jayakody advancing slowly forward, towards me, and his little eyes have come out of the sockets and flash with cold undiluted anger and I get up and the uproar begins to recede like an ebbing wave and now the garden lizard is hissing and blowing and Tony moves sideways with fangs bared and barking wildly and Mr. Jayakody has stopped right near me and he pushes his dark black ugly face right up and I could almost hear his breathing, heavy and angry, and the black dragon is swishing his scaly tail and Tony is dangerously close to the monster and the barking becomes fierce and desperate but in the classroom now there is an awesome silence and I keep looking helplessly at the dark face and the tiny eyes in front of me and then there is a blinding flash and a cracking sound and I close my eyes and hold my cheek and slowly an excruciating pain begins on my lower jaw and spreads all over my face like scalding water and all I hear is Tony barking furiously.

The whistle was a hoarse metallic honk more like the cry of a dying animal and the train that crossed the road at right angles in front of me was not small; it was a broad gauge train coming from Homagama and the amber-colored wagons with bands of white and ash on them were drawn by a cream-painted electric engine that looked like a rectangular box — not quite my idea of a train, which is a black barrel with a red protruding muzzle like a dragon's mouth, a funnel and two cupolas on top breathing fire and smoke and that long-lingering-sad whistle. The Maharagama Halt — once-upon-a-time a wood cabin on a long platform like Udahamulla — has become a station with a two-story main block and an overhead pedestrian walk — crude and ugly with its plain walls disfigured by huge spray-gun scrawls and election posters. Once the train cleared the level crossing, the motor traffic started to move and I drove slowly over the rail track, which stood out from the worn-out and broken asphalt layer at the intersection. I shifted gear and proceeded carefully through the milling crowd and the vans parked all over — this was an ancient path that stretched from Kotte all the way to Piliyandala through the paddy fields of Erawwala and beyond that to Rayigama but now broken up and obliterated over long patches by the twentieth-century network of roads crisscrossing the Kelani Valley and what is left begins on the old road near the Maharagama Railway Station and remained, till the early eighties, a quiet rural byway, a little more than a cart track, when for some not well-known reason the first few hundred yards came to be lined on either side by hundreds of tiny stalls selling ready-made clothes turned out of cut-away cloth-ends collected in bulk from the big garment factories, and vans and lorries would come from far and wide throughout the week for wholesale purchases and large crowds throng the stalls till late in the night for bargains in anything from bras, panties, skirts, blouses, shorts, shirts, and household linen.

It was early April in the year 1996 and the New Year rush

was on and I was beginning to regret having taken this route—
a month had gone since I completed work on *Pitagamkarayo*
and during that period I had been trying to trace the landscape
of my childhood beneath the changes of the last forty-six years
and today I went through the site of the now vanished village
of Egodawatta looking for places I could recognize—they were
few and far between and every nook and corner was covered
with ugly box-like structures—and then I crossed the paddy
field—where the last scene of *Pitagamkarayo* was shot—along
the new connecting byway and it was around four in the afternoon but the sun was bright and harsh like it was noontime
and it was after the harvest and the plots were bare and there
was no water in the canal—my friend GR (none other than
Theliya of Egodawatta of my childhood who went away to
Grandpass to attend a Colombo school and who has now
become an actor of repute and still very much in touch with
the village though living elsewhere) tells me that the effluence
from the Arpico factory at Nawinna has killed all the fish—and
I reached the Maharagama-Dehiwela road, turned left, and
skirting the Boralesgamuwa Tank—only a mud hole now where
buffaloes wallow at all times of the day—I came to Maharagama; I had planned to reach Depanama via the High Level
Road—along the same route I walked with Tony—but on an
impulse crossed the High Level Road on to the Old Road and
turned left near the railway station, which is how I found myself
caught in the rush on Pamunuwa Road—yes, that is the name
of this ancient road, which after about half a mile from the
station moves along one boundary of the Kendahena Estate
and which land stretches on the other side all the way to one
border of Depanama where there is the story of a murdered
woman tapper whose ghost walks under the rubber trees at
high noon; the Pamunuwa road, after skirting the edge of the
rubber land, passes a junction and proceeds straight to the bund

of the Diyawanna Oya at Kotte but a branch road turns right at the junction and moves in a wide crescent to cross a paddy field and reach the Depanama road a good half a mile from the Pannipitiya Railway Station.

I crawled out of the rush and began to drive more easily along the road now widened to contain the traffic cutting through from Maharagama to the new capital of Sri Jayawardenapura and kept looking constantly on my right to see the beginnings of the old rubber estate but soon discovered that Kendahena, like Egodawatta, too had disappeared; where stood neat rows of rubber trees forming clear lanes between and that crossed the terraced ground sloping gently towards the paddy fields, now there were hundreds of flat roofs vying to rise above each other and from the rooftops bristled TV antennae like trees in a dead forest and the boxlike concrete houses sitting behind high walls in narrow enclosures looked dead too, cold and lifeless, and I cruised along, took a right turn at the junction and began a slow descent. The road twisted and turned but continued to go down until it dipped sharply to cross a narrow strip of paddy field—this was a kind of neck in the valley of the field that broadened out on the left to a vast expanse spreading all the way through Battaramulla and Kaduwela to the banks of the Kelani River, and on the right it crept between Kendahena on the right and on the left Weragala Estate—another piece of rubber land where I roamed with Tony picking pod shells and collecting panel scrap to make cricket balls with—to reach a dead-end at the foot of an old quarry, and the small house we occupied at Depanama before we left for Egodawatta stood somewhere on the slope to the fields between Kendahena and the quarry; Geera Atha who would bring milk in the morning and who lived in an old house—the house with the two framed rabbits—closer to where I was standing now, on the road over the neck of the

paddy field—would tell Mother that when he was a little boy—
"long before the Jubilee" as he put it and he meant Queen Victoria's Golden Jubilee in 1887, and for him everything
happened before or after this event—this part of the valley was
a tank, and listening to him I thought this surely must be true
because during the monsoon rains in July through August the
paddy field would turn into a lake and the three brothers—
Piyasena, Jayasena, and Jinadasa who lived by the edge of the
quarry—would teach me how to make a boat with plantain-
tree trunks fixed together with thick pieces of bamboo and go
rowing in the water and Tony who couldn't get in the water
kept barking madly from high ground, and where I was standing now and where the road crossed the narrow strip of paddy
land must have been the bund of the now-vanished tank.

Minutes later I fell into the Borella-Pannipitiya road at Polwatta where the paddy field comes around once more to cross
the road in its spread towards Hokandara and where on Easter
Sunday in April 1942 a British Hurricane fighter plane crash-
landed during the Japanese air raid and I still have a clear rec-
ollection of seeing the wounded pilot being taken on a hackery
driven by carter John along the road in front of the house by
the fir trees where we lived—the split-level house with the bay
windows on the upper level from where I would watch the blue
mountains over the trees—and the white man was clinging to
the backrest of the hackery like a frightened monkey with a
large crowd following behind—and Mother was pretty sure
I had constructed the whole scene from hearsay in later years
because in 1942 I was three years old and according to her it
is not possible to remember that far back and over the years
I came to doubt it myself, but now I remembered the scene
once more and it seemed quite real, and if it was otherwise like
Mother suspected, it didn't seem to matter anymore.

I turned right and the road kept climbing gradually until

a few hundred yards ahead of me at the end of the rise I saw the co-op store with its low flat-tiled roof after forty-six years. On the right of the road just before the store was where the entrance to Weragala Estate stood in those days—a wooden gate and beyond that a long gravel drive that went through the neat rows of rubber trees; all that had vanished and once more I saw the flat roofs and the TV antennae; from the past only the pylon remained towering like a giant skeleton and I remembered how they laid the overhead cables cutting a swath through the rubber trees and in the thick vegetation in the village beyond how men dangled from the top of steel girders making me feel dizzy, the labor gangs singing in chorus as they dragged the heavy cables and the huge drums revolving as the cables uncoiled, "Heeye" they chorused and then came some strange words in a raplike incantation and then once more "Heeye" in a monotonous rhythm and the gravelly voices making me sleepy in the noonday heat. Opposite the co-op store the old house where the Weerakodys lived and where I learned my first songs stood unchanged inside the large garden and I heard Nirmali Akka sing "Ase madhura jeevanaye geetha namu ama dahare . . . " with the archway behind her in the hall of the house draped with multicolored saris to form a stage backdrop because it was a house concert, and then a half-built house on the same compound by the edge of the road where once Appuhamy's wife and who was Geera Atha's daughter used to make hoppers in the open front of another house of wattle-and-daub with a thatched roof and which has given way to the new structure closed in front; an old woman with gray hair and wearing that long gown buttoned up in front and known once-upon-a-time as the "kimono" and now as the "housecoat" stood on a side between the unplastered wall and the fence and I guessed that to be "Chutti" who was Appuhamy's youngest daughter and who as a little girl worked for us as a domestic help in the big house; I wanted to stop the car and talk to her and ask her whether she knew who I am but felt inhibited; there was something forced about the situation like something from a bad piece of fiction and I shifted my gaze to the next point beyond, and there was the big house, the one with two levels and the dining room with the bay windows, the house where Tony came into our family as a roly-poly-fluffy pup; the fir trees were gone and so was the bougainvillea creeper that crawled all over the fence in a riot of crimson, but the palm tree covering the facade of the portico was still there and I looked up to the crest of the roof over the portico where two hips met in an inverted V and where perched in those days a sculpted heron—I could never accept that bird as a dummy and would gaze at it expecting it to fly away any moment and each morning I would come out to check whether the bird was still there—and now at last it has flown away. The parapet wall still enclosed the garden and ran parallel with the road-front and still looked good and strong but the gate was different: instead of the blue wooden gate with the grill of the rising sun, now there was a crude iron frame with crisscrossing bars; on the other side of the road the high croton fence that screened the school was gone and a new building closer to the road covered the older one and the huge jak tree that rose above the tiled roof in those days was gone too but now once more I was in the big house and standing in the veranda and the babble of children's voices came from beyond the thick wall of croton bushes and some voices were singing and they were heard above the others but the words weren't clear, yet the melody held me as it rose and fell like slowly overlapping waves and I held Tony in my hands and he was warm against my chest and the singing rose in a crescendo up and up above the croton bushes like a swirling mist and then wrapped itself around the huge canopy of the jak tree like a cloud and scattered in a flock of white birds over and around the fir trees until the Little Train whistled sadly in the distance and I woke up thinking it was morning when it was late afternoon and I was wondering why Prema the servant girl was not sweeping the room and why the light coming through the window was so pale and then I heard the toot of the car horn and rushing to the window saw the red car with the long bonnet turn into the side road and Guneris was running to open the corrugated iron gate at the lower level and I came running out of the room and crossed the hall and went hippity-hop down the wooden stairway and Father came out of the garage loaded with parcels and as he dropped them and carried me in his arms the roly-poly-fluffy pup started yapping continuously from somewhere.

There was an old man with gray hair on his chest standing by the bamboo wicket in the compound right next to the big house and I thought that was for sure Edmund, the big boy next door who taught me to make trains out of empty match boxes half a century ago; he was much older to me even then and now he looked quite old as he stood there, short and stocky, staring vacantly at the road, and I slowed down and grinned through the closed shutter and he bent down slightly to look at me and I think he thought I was going to speak to him and almost took a step forward but there came within me that inhibition now almost like a fear—it was a strange feeling that held me back from making contact with these people from the past and looking back now I remember it was like wanting to hang on to a dream and not wanting to wake up. I moved on and from the mirror I saw Edmund standing there looking slightly confused and receding into the background and now I was passing the spot where on the left of the road was a patch of jungle and in a corner—in those days—was a little hut where lived Roma the madman and his mother was a frail looking woman with brown eyes and beyond their hut was a large tree and from that point onwards the land sloped down through the woods to the paddy field and from somewhere within that dark wood—once more in those days—a tall dark man would emerge carrying a gun—he had bloodshot eyes and his body was as black as charcoal and most of the time he carried a dead rabbit or a mouse deer dripping with blood and his name was Dimitiyas. But now the land has been cleared and some Buddhist center was being built there. After this spot was the land where Mary Akka had her hopper boutique though the place hasn't changed much except there were three small houses built out of earth bricks where earlier there was only one. I slowed down once again and looked to my right and there by the old dilapidated house was the narrow gravel path that led to the small house below the quarry and above the paddy field and from the back of which you looked straight towards Weragala Estate where I roamed with Tony picking pod shells and panel scrap and where Geera Atha would come each morning with two bottles of fresh cow's milk, warm and straight from the udder and where during the monsoon rains there was a lake where I would go rowing in boats made of plantain-tree trunks and from high ground Tony would bark furiously as we rowed and splashed.

The path that went cutting through high ground on either side was like the way into a cave and then I remembered that the middle stretch of that path was dark and gloomy at all times and I was scared—in those days—to walk there even in broad daylight, but today there was a different kind of fear as I kept looking at the beginning of that path; from where I stood I could see the point where the path dipped and disappeared as if it fell into an abyss and that was exactly the spot Tony came charging from somewhere and fell at my feet in that final meeting of ours and I longed to walk up to that spot and then go sailing into the abyss to emerge once more into the open near the old quarry but then would everything be the same as when I left forty-six years ago? Will the road go by the house, still on a higher level, and then turn right abruptly to avoid the little patch of wood just before Mr. Lawrence Perera's house and from which place would emerge rabbits, polecats, and even mouse deer to be chased by Tony through the marshland down below and across the field all the way to Weragala Estate on the other side? Would Geera Atha still emerge through the mist early in the morning, his head wrapped in sarong and advance slowly like a bogeyman with two bottles of cow's milk in hand? Would all that be gone like the rubber trees of Kendahena and Weragala Estate giving way to flat concrete rooftops sprouting the dead plants of TV antennae?

A man began emerging from the abyss; his head kept bobbing up and down for some time and then came the rest of the man, tall and strongly built and dressed in a white gauze banian and a checked sarong; he came walking with a swagger like the way toughs move and his manner changed immediately when he saw me standing by the car; his hands stopped swinging and his pace slowed down before he paused at the top of the road; I removed my dark glasses because I thought I recognized him; he could be Jayasena—the second of the three brothers who taught me to row a boat in the rain waters—and I became more certain as I crossed the road and came closer to him; he kept looking at me with suspicion and I thought there was fear in his eyes too and I smiled, trying to look friendly, but he simply kept looking at me until I asked him whether he was Jayasena and his eyes grew big and his mouth opened slightly and he nodded rather vaguely, never removing his sharp eyes from me for a moment, and then I told him who I was, and he just stared at me blankly and I went on describing many things in detail right down to the boats we made out of plantain-tree trunks and his eyes grew bigger and his mouth opened wider as if he had seen a ghost but there was no recognition in those eyes where lurked some fear and then he spoke and he said something to the effect that he was Jayasena all right and he also had two brothers by names of Piyasena and Jinadasa but he does not remember me nor any of the things I described and after a moment of uneasy silence when neither of us spoke but kept looking at each other stupidly, I said it was all right, that maybe I had made a mistake and though that was a stupid thing to say, he looked relieved and quickly turned around and started walking away along the road towards from where I came and I crossed the road and got into the car and I looked in the mirror and saw the man walking away and he did not look back even once and I thought maybe if I spoke to Chutti and Edmund earlier on the road I would have had a similar response and I was feeling empty and for the first time having serious doubts about many things. Now it was very late in the afternoon and the amber light on tree tops was receding fast and I wanted to be back home.

The Pannipitiya Railway Station rose up from behind the embankment and it remained unchanged right down to the name board where the English letters were still on top as it used to be—Pannipitiya. Sixty feet above sea level—the part about the sea level was only in English; the cactus bushes however were gone and the embankment didn't look as steep as I remembered and the railway lines had been widened into the broad gauge and there was a green tat hanging over the balcony of the Station Master's quarters upstairs (during Mr. Samarasinghe's time the balcony was open) but the station in its main contours remained the same and was drawing me back into the dream and as I stood on the edge of the embankment I began to hear the tennis ball hit the racquet thuk thuk thik thok and I remembered a feeling I had that continued for an year or so even after we left Depanama; I felt that everything

TISSA ABEYSEKARA   *69*

that happened after we left the big house by the fir trees and with that sculpted heron on the crest of the portico roof was only a bad dream and I would get up one morning under the pink mosquito net and Prema the servant girl would come quietly and roll it up and the bright morning light would streak into the room on the upper level of the big house and Tony the roly-poly-fluffy pup would come bouncing and jump into the bed and start licking my face and I would hold him warm against my chest and go out of the room to stand by the bay windows in the dining room and Mother would be down in the quadrangle wearing that peacock-blue wraparound kimono with the red dragon on the back and I would look up and beyond the trees and beyond the paddy field and above the green haze and see the clear line of the blue mountains far far away and now the red Jaguar with the long bonnet was coming slowly down the side road and Guneris was opening the gate of corrugated iron on the lower level and I was running hippity-hop down the stairway and Father was coming out of the garage dropping his bags and lifting me up in his arms and the roly-poly-fluffy pup was yapping continuously and then there was the sad whistle and it merged with the hoarse and anguished cry of a dying animal and the broad gauge train with its boxlike electric engine pulling the amber-colored wagons with white and ash bands rolled into the station; no one got down and no one boarded and someone in rolled-up shirt sleeves and wearing no cap walked lazily across the platform with the tablet held loosely like a shopping bag. The hoarse metallic whistle sounded again and the train was pulling out and the roly-poly-fluffy pup continued to yap yap yap from somewhere but now it was nothing mischievous or joyous; it was the plaintive cry of a chained dog trying desperately to be free.

Poor Young Man

—

A Requiem

In my office a framed quote hangs on the wall. When I sit at my desk it is on my left. I can see it across the space between my desk and the middle of the left wall beyond the frame of a curtained window and the air-conditioning unit below it. At that distance I cannot read the text within the frame, even though the print is fairly big and bold. But that does not matter, not only because I know what is there by memory, but because I look at it as a picture and not something to be read word by word and sentence by sentence from left to right. I read it differently, because for me the meaning lay elsewhere. Each morning as I enter the room and walk from the door up to my desk, I have to pass this framed quote on the wall. It is on my right, and I pass very close to it because the space between one end of the large conference table, which is placed across the room and across from the wall, is very narrow, and I must walk through that. I pause for a moment each time I move past this spot out of some secret compulsion, and even then, when I stand very close to it, I do not read the text. I hold it in my view like I am looking at a picture, and there is an uprush of feeling within me, both warm and sad.

When I turned twenty-one my father presented me with a book. It was a big old book with a discolored jacket frayed at the edges and a piece torn away at the back. Father would have most certainly purchased it at a secondhand bookstore. The first owner's name had been crossed out to make it unreadable. Maybe it was Father who had done it. But he had not inscribed anything, which he normally did whenever he gave me a book. Father had given me many books at various times in my life from the time I started to read. There was one I received when I was around ten — one of the last books he could afford brand new, and I think it was a novel by Dickens — where he had inscribed in his neat and very readable hand the whole of Polonius's advice to Laertes from *Hamlet*. So, for a moment, I wondered why Father had not written anything in this book which, incidentally, was also the last book he ever gave me. However, such things had ceased to be of any great importance to me at that point in my life. I had been steadily moving away from Father's influence, and also his authority, since I reached my middle teens.

At nineteen I had lost my innocence, dropped out of high school, and was spending most of my time away from home. I came home only when I needed a change of clothes, to get some sleep, and also because, in spite of everything, Mother was always waiting for her only son. I hardly spoke with Father. Though there were times I felt he wanted to talk to me, I would avoid conversation by giving curt monosyllabic answers. He understood and stopped talking.

It was during this period that I turned twenty-one and Father presented me with that big old book with a torn jacket. It was a biography of Napoleon by a little-known writer, J.S.C. Abbott, in nine hundred–odd pages of small print.

Father had many ideals. Almost all of them were European. Napoleon Bonaparte topped the list. From the point in time where my memory begins, a print of a painting of Napoleon hung in Father's study. It showed Napoleon astride his favorite charger, Marengo, at the famous Battle of Jena, or was it Austerlitz? This picture fitted well with the scale of things when we were living in the big house with many rooms and Father's study was at one end of the long veranda, which ran along two sides of the drawing room in the shape of an L. The study had large bay windows, and placed in one corner was a writing table with a baize-lined top. When we moved from that house to a smaller one, and then to still smaller ones in rapid succession, and the books began to disappear—I was to learn later that Father kept selling them to keep us from going hungry, and sometimes even to pay the rent—Napoleon on his charger began to look a bit funny in the small rooms that doubled for a bedroom and a study. In the fifties, when we hit rock bottom and began to live in a single room sharing a common veranda, Napoleon disappeared completely. Mother may have thrown it away secretly, or even destroyed it. She was getting increasingly annoyed and impatient with the way Father clung desperately to certain things; he wouldn't eat with his fingers and insisted on his fork and spoon; it was sad to see him eating very basic meals Mother put on the table like it was a four-course dinner. He had stopped bathing because he could not draw water from the deep well. He tried once and dropped the bucket inside the well, rope and all. All this made Mother furious. She was angry when he sat down to his meals with labored ceremony, and she walked about like an agitated hen deliberately making distracting noises and movements whenever Father sat down with a book in some corner of the cramped spaces we lived in. Poor Mother—fun-loving, mischievous, constantly teasing the servants who simply adored her, mock-fighting with her only child, singing softly and constantly to herself, beautiful, all once-upon-a-time. She had become ill-tempered, sour, sad, and withdrawn.

Time dragged along like a broken animal through long days in cramped spaces with the tension between Mother's ill temper and Father's abnormal, sometimes frightening calm (he was deep within a mental cave like some hibernating animal) when two sisters arrived within three years of each other—one eleven years my junior, and the other thirteen; hardships continued. Perhaps they became greater because there were more mouths to feed now, but a few things changed for the better: We moved into a small yet whole house where I had a room—the one adjoining the small veranda—all to myself, because I was a big boy now.

This was the time I began to get restless and was moving away from Father. Then one day, in what seemed like a long time after I left school, I turned twenty-one.

The previous night had gone on into the wee hours of the morning, and I had come home after a week and was still lying in bed at nine in the morning when Father came into the room and pushed open the window. It was a small window with two unpainted wooden panes and covered with a half-curtain of cheap cloth. As Father stood there with the late morning light playing on his face, he looked sad, and I sat up in bed. I felt vaguely uncomfortable lying in bed while Father stood by that little window with that cheap curtain and those crude wooden panes looking sad. It was also a reflex action, because in spite of the growing estrangement between us, I still couldn't be indifferent to Father's presence; I stood up whenever he came into wherever I was, fell silent if I had been talking, or simply moved away. Was this some kind of habit coming down from childhood?

As a kid I followed Mother and the way she behaved in Father's presence. She never sat with him except when asked to do so by him, and that was only when there were visitors, and she remained silent whenever he was talking. She wouldn't do anything without his approval, and whenever anything had to be done, it was always a matter of "Let's ask Father," or if she was talking with someone else it was, "I'll have to ask *Him*." (She always referred to him as *Him* and never by name.) Sometimes *He* was "This one's father," the "this one" being me. I also loved *Him* in another way and waited for him to come home. I don't think he came home every day, and there were days when

I knew Father would be coming. I knew it from the time I woke up in the morning by the way Mother moved around, by the way the servants were busier than usual, and later in the day by the cooking smells coming from the kitchen downstairs. Father would toot the horn of his red Jaguar with that long bonnet a long way before he reached the gate, and I would get all excited like a puppy.

All this had changed over the years. By the time I reached sixteen, home was a two-room house with leaking roofs and dirty-paint-flaking walls with the smell of unwashed clothes; cheap milchard rice cooking on smoky wood fires with the smelly smoke clinging to everything and always lurking in the cramped spaces; moldy sweat-stained bed linen, washed per-haps once a month because there wasn't enough linen to change the beds more than that; Mother looking harassed, worn out and constantly edgy; Father lying in bed, sometimes for days, unwashed and getting up only to eat whatever Mother put on the table, or just seated on the old chair in the veranda staring vacantly, or sometimes gone for days and returning home late in the night, his clothes soiled after being in them for days and smelling of sweat; and Mother complaining of all the trouble she had to go through to feed three children, and Father pre-tending not to hear, and Mother getting angry, and then Father telling her in his low monotone, which never went up nor down under any circumstances, that all this happened because of her bad luck, and it was enough that he stuck with her, and Mother beginning to cry, and then the two kid sisters waking up and beginning to cry because Mother is crying, and I am listen-ing to all this from my room, which adjoins the veranda and is separated from the room inside by a wall not quite reaching up to the roof, and I could hear everything happening on the other side—and then I am waiting for the next moment of this drama like the fixed text of a play: the loud banging of two doors—

the only expression of feeling on the part of Father, which is unusual because he is normally quite unflappable, even gentle in his actions, so much so that I think it to be a trick to wake me up for the next moment of the action that needs my participation—as Father walks out, first from the room, and then from the narrow sitting area that opens out into the veranda. Then I hear him walk down the three steps of rough cement, and now his worn-out shoes make a soft dragging sound on the gravel footpath dissolving in the still night. Now I wait for the next inevitable act: Mother taps on my door, and when I open it she wants me to go fetch Father. It is nearly midnight, or perhaps past midnight, and the two kids are crying because Mother is still crying, and I put on a shirt and walk through the dark unlit gravel road, which reaches a broader one, and I know Father will be there at the intersection. I know he invariably stops here because each time this happens I have found him standing there like a ghost silhouetted against the pale white of the sky—here the road, the small one, which I am on, crests an incline to meet the broader one, and beyond that is a treeless moor rising gently, creating a low skyline. I think Father always knew I would come—he made sure by banging the doors loud enough to wake me up, in case I was asleep, and I think he wasn't sure I was asleep or not; this makes me feel something like resentment against Father, first for causing this uncomfortable situation, and then for dragging me into it; I feel kind of cheated, manipulated. But somewhere within me is also the vague fear that I may not find him standing there, and that he may have vanished into the night, never to be seen again. In those days that fear was constantly within me. I now think it was something connected with the excitement of seeing him come home after many days in his red Jaguar during the better times at the big house with the large veranda and the office room with the bay windows and the baize-topped writing desk in a corner with the painting of Napoleon on his charger at the Battle of Jena—or was it Austerlitz? In that big house Father was someone who came and went, never permanently there, someone I wasn't quite sure of. Hence, there was this constant fear of losing him. Now, looking back, I think it was this fear that slowly developed into resentment. It was not very pleasant to be scared all the time that your father may suddenly leave you, never to return; that one day, however much you waited, he wouldn't return.

This fear made me tense each day as evening came and the narrow road in front of our sad little house was flowing with people coming home after work. Father never came home before nightfall, and for me evenings in those days were always heavy with foreboding. This feeling, whatever it could be called, matured into an anger as I reached my middle teens, which was when I first began to want to run away. I was constantly running away somewhere in my thoughts, in my dreams, and I was fast losing interest in school.

School was painful.

School fees were always not paid for months, and it was painful to have your name read in class for nonpayment of fees, and when you were in arrears for over three months you were sent to the office and then sent home with a letter. I was never sent home like that because the principal had been Father's classmate in some big Colombo school, which made it even more painful. When I was sent to him he looked at me as if I was a big bother. He would tell me to tell Father that in spite of everything, he took me into the school because Father was a friend who was now down and out in life, but that this— meaning the school—was not a charitable institution. That "in spite of everything" always bothered me; he was obviously hinting at something.

It was also painful not to have all the books you needed in

class, painful when you wore the same pair of tussore trousers day after day, and sometimes with a damp smell clinging to them because Mother would wash them once in two days in the afternoons, and during the rainy season they wouldn't properly dry in the morning when I had to wear them. It was painful to avoid the company of girls because wearing the same trousers every day made you lack confidence, and also because you didn't smell of Old Spice like Daluwatta, Dabare, Reggie, and Donald from the hostel did—hostellers always wore satin drill trousers and Arrow shirts with stiff collars and smelled of Old Spice. It was also painful when the games master said you bowl well and could be in the cricket pool, but Mother said there's no money for "all that fancy gear" they wanted if I was to play cricket. Secretly I began to hold Father responsible for all the pain and humiliation I was going through. There were also times I felt mad at him, like when he couldn't give me money for a school picnic, and I began fussing, and he told me of some fellow named Babington Lord Macaulay who, when he was a poor kid and his mother said there was nothing to eat for dinner, replied, "Ambition shall be my bread."

I hardly noticed my sisters. They were living in a world of their own, far away from me in age, and I suppose totally free of the things that troubled me. They were both born after we became poor, and they knew of no other life than the one they were born to and grew up in. They were sweet, uncomplicated kids who attended the village school. It was Mother who insisted on sending them to some school that was available, because she didn't want her two daughters staying at home long after school-going age like her son did. Father didn't like this arrangement; he said he didn't want his children to get mixed up with what he referred to as the village "riffraff." But he had another reason, and at sixteen, I was to discover it.

In those days—that was before I became sixteen and dis-covered this "something"—I don't think I hated Father. It was more a feeling of being let down by someone you had placed all your faith in, someone you believed to be strong, powerful, and clever. When that someone lies in bed unwashed, and for days with everyone else like him going to work in the morn-ing, something begins to happen within you; when that some-one is gone for days, and Mother sends me to her sister to borrow money, and when that sister and her children were not allowed in our house when we were rich once-upon-a-time on Father's orders because Mother's people were considered not socially acceptable to him, something begins to crumble within you.

Then one day—I can only remember that it was during the school holidays in April, because Mother had been getting agi-tated that the Sinhala New Year was only a week ahead and there was no money for anything—Mother left in the morning to her sister's place with my two kid sisters, obviously to bor-row some money, and I was alone in the house with nothing to do and was moving around feeling restless. I can remember that a quiet rage was building up within me, but I don't remem-ber why; it was like when you want to smash up something, or scream at the top of your voice in shocking filth. I walked into the dirty and messy bedroom where Father, Mother, and my two sisters slept in two beds, and where in a corner stood Father's writing desk—that baize-topped table, which was one of the few items left from the days in the big house. There was in that desk a row of drawers on the right as you sit, over which a wooden flap closed and that could be locked. Once that wooden flap was locked, none of the drawers could be opened. It was a device to lock all four drawers—yes, there were four drawers—with one key. As a child, these four drawers and the wooden flap that closed over them had made me curious. It was always Father who opened these drawers, and I think he had the key. I hadn't questioned that. There are some things like that in a child's life—things inaccessible, taken for granted, and never questioned. The set of four drawers in Father's writing desk, which could be closed with a single wooden flap, was one such thing in my childhood. But on that day—the day Mother had gone with my two kid sisters, leaving me alone in the house—I was no longer a child. I hadn't been feeling or behaving like a child in a long time, and on that day—the day I was all alone in that house—I was mad at something. Inside that bedroom, with dirty smelly clothes lying all over, my attention was drawn to that set of drawers in Father's writing desk, locked with a single wooden flap as it had always been. That day I felt it was jeering at me, making me feel helpless. The entire writing desk, with its baize top and the notebooks arranged so neatly on either side and the locked set of drawers jeering at me inside this miserable room, said many things. Slowly the anger building up within me began to concentrate on the lock.

I wanted to break it open.

I didn't know how to break open a lock, but I had seen people do it with a safety pin or a hairpin. It took me some time to find a pin; what I found was a hairpin, the kind like an elongated *V* with wavy wrinkles on either side.

In my life there had been no miracles. There were only accidents, and they had never been in my favor. What happened that day with the lock was definitely an accident, but for the first and perhaps the last time in my life, it was in my favor — or was it really? I wonder sometimes now. No sooner had I inserted the pin and turned it gently inside that the lock opened.

For an average teenager, secretly opening Father's drawers is no big deal. But on that day, as the lock clicked open in my father's secret set of drawers, I remember feeling jumpy inside like something was going to explode. Even today, opening a drawer makes me nervous. The genesis of that feeling is in the moment I opened Father's set of secret drawers. Or is it really? Sometimes I think it all began much earlier, in that fear that Father would disappear one day, that he is not a permanent item in my life. Now when did that feeling begin? I can't be certain. It was in the air around me since memory began, in the way Mother moved around when Father was there and when Father was not there, in the way the horn of the red Jaguar with the long bonnet sounded as it took the turn near the railway station, which was a good three minutes before it reached the gate of the big house by the fir trees, from the back of which and through the bay windows in the upper floor I could see the blue mountains in the distance, and the Little Train whistled somewhere. This feeling began growing like a fever as we moved into smaller houses and Napoleon disappeared because Father couldn't have a separate study and Mother became ill-tempered. The feeling persisted within me, and without, in Mother's edgy ways, in Father's alarming silence as he lay in bed or sat in the chair unwashed, and with Mother moving around registering her protest in many and tiny different ways. Like a bad smell coming from a source I couldn't locate. Now what happened on that day—the day I broke open the lock of Father's set of drawers—was that I located it. I knew it was locked up somewhere within those four drawers, and I knew it was not something pleasant. That's what made me jumpy.

The top drawer was full of diaries. Thin ones, fat ones, small ones, big ones—they were of various colors, but since all the colors were of dark shades now gone pale with time, they looked the same. All the diaries were strictly arranged in chronological order. The first one was of the year 1915. He would have been fifteen then—he was born in 1900 and was very happy he managed to squeeze himself into the reign of Queen Victoria by one year. He had told me that he kept a diary since he was nine, but in that drawer the daily chronicle of his life began six years later. The first years of the narrative were gone. Perhaps he hadn't preserved them. My hand moved swiftly over the years and stopped at 1939, The year I was born. It was a small book with a brick-red cover. Each page was divided into two days, and I began seeking the day I was born. 7 May 1939. The story of my birth has become part of family myth. I had heard it being related by Mother, Father, and Aunt Soma—Mother's best friend who was heavy with child herself and who stood by as I arrived ahead of schedule by a week and after much labor—from four different angles, *Rashomon*-like. According to Mother, she had felt the symptoms in the morning but kept them to herself; Father had gone on some business matter to Ratnapura two days earlier, and before going he had got the clearance from Mother that my arrival wouldn't be for another week. Towards afternoon, when the pains increased, she sent word to Soma. At this point Aunt Soma takes over the narrative: It was raining heavily. She had to walk nearly a mile and on the way got drenched. Near the house where I was born there was a railway crossing. A train had stopped, blocking the way, and the engine was right in the middle of the crossing. Aunt Soma paused here, her sari wet and clinging to her, revealing the contours of a heavily pregnant woman. The engine driver kept feasting his eyes on Aunt Soma (she was only eighteen at the time and quite pretty) and she felt—as she related gleefully to me much later, when I was big enough to hear such comments—as if she was standing there stark naked.

Night. Maharagama Railway Station. It's still raining, and the Little Train—thus named because it was a small train almost like a toy that plied a narrow gauge railway line running from

Colombo to the southwestern flank of the central hills across the valley of the Kelani River—steams into the Maharagama Station, a wayside halt with a little cabin serving as the Station Master's office. It was the first westbound train in four days, since the monsoon rains had flooded the valley and all traffic had come to a standstill. Father comes in the train. In spite of Mother's assurance, he had been anxious to get back. Leaving his car at the Ratnapura Rest House, he had taken the first train back. He claims he was the only passenger to get off the train here. Through the rain and in the dark he saw someone standing on the platform, and he was holding an umbrella. Father walks up and recognizes him. He was the young boy who lived next door, and he offers Father the umbrella. The conversation, as recalled by Father over and over again, varied only slightly at each telling, and went something like this:

"We heard a train was coming from Ratnapura."
   "Yes."
   "And I was asked to wait."
   "Wait for whom?"
   "Wait for you."
   "Why?"
   Already alarm bells were ringing within Father—or so he has told me many times, and the way he told me, it must have been true.
   "A son was born."
   "A son was born?"
   "Yes, Sir. A son was born."
   Silence.
   "A son was born this evening."
   "A son was born to whom?"
   "To the Lady."
   Silence.

"A son was born to your Lady, Sir."

Silence.

"This evening, Sir."

Father drops the umbrella in his hand and begins to run along the rain-swept narrow platform. He gets on to the gravel road that is all soft with rain and continues running through the rain and the mud and the slush all the way and stands shivering and dripping by Mother's bedside.

That was the scene as recalled from Father's angle. I had heard it so often, and narrated by Father with so much feeling and description, never varying in detail, that it remained in my memory like a scene from a movie I had seen many times. I could see the rain falling all over, the Little Train coming through the late-evening dark and pulling to a halt by the stone-paved platform with puddles, the steam from the engine, white and hissing like a snake, blending with the spray of the slow rain reflected in the fierce glare of the train's headlamps, the station at the far end of the platform, small and square like a log cabin, Father getting off the train, the lone passenger on the platform, a man with an umbrella waiting for him in the dark, the conversation — clipped, short sentences, tense with the impending news of my birth held back almost by dramatic design — then the moment of realization, the shocking pleasure, the uninterrupted run along the pavement, through the rain and the mud and the slush.

As I searched nervously for the entry in Father's diary for Sunday, 7 May 1939, I suppose it was natural for me to have expected something of the excitement and the drama of that day, as it lay in my memory based on Father's telling of it, to be there, recorded. What I found in the half page allocated for that day in the small pocket diary with a brick-colored cover now faded, were three sentences:

Returned from Ratnapura by train after being held up for three days.
It has been raining heavily.
Agnes has given birth to a baby boy.

At sixteen I could not have understood all the implications of those three lines in Father's diary. But I knew that the entry avoided many things by calculation, and in doing so denies me something. There was a vast gap between Father's story of the moment of my birth, as recounted by him orally to me, and what has been committed to ink in that small diary. It was a cold dry statement bleached of all connotation and feeling. It takes no responsibility for what has happened. Agnes could be any woman who has given birth to a child, and there isn't the vaguest hint of paternity.

I could articulate all of this so clearly only in retrospect. At the moment of confrontation it confused me. Behind that confusion I could remember a dull pain, something that felt like a heaviness in the chest slowly working upwards to the head.

The drawer is closed, slowly, and the second drawer opened, equally slowly.

I see a metal box, sea-green in color, its paint mottled and beginning to flake slightly. The box has a handle, chrome-plated, which once-upon-a-time would have shone like silver. Now it lies on its side, looking passive and harmless. There is also a small keyhole. But the box is not locked, because when I lift the handle and pull it up, the lid opens, without a fuss.

On top I see a blue piece of paper neatly folded, and I find it to be the receipt from the shipping line through which Father had booked his passage to England. Beneath that is another document, vaguely cream in color, and it is from Jesus College, Oxford, confirming the enrollment of Arthur Solomon de Fonseka—that was Father—as a student. I remembered seeing these documents earlier; Father had always produced them as evidence of his unrealized trip to England and a prospective career at Oxford. After a brilliant secondary school career at one of the elite schools in Colombo, where he carried prizes for history and Latin year after year, he was booked to go to Oxford. All clever young men of his social class in Colombo had to go to an English university. It was mandatory, like going to school when you were five years of age, though if you were to go to England, as they put it, you had to do exceptionally well at secondary school, and your parents had to be rich. Father had dutifully qualified, and his family was rich, and everything was ready for him to go to England. Father's planned trip to England, and how it had to be cancelled just the very day he was to set sail, was another dramatic strand in the family chronicle.

All the key relatives were visited in the week prior to the departure, and their blessings obtained, the necessary religious rituals for good luck and protection performed, the bags were packed, and there was a dinner for the members of the inner family—some of them had arrived from afar to see Artie—this was a shortened form for Arthur, the name which Father's family and closest friends called him—off to England. The last thing to do before retiring to bed was to have a very personal conversation with his father, which lasted well over half an hour. Whenever Father related the story, he kept this detail to the last, not because it was the last thing he did for the day before going to bed in the story, but because he, in his style of storytelling, used this trick of withholding a key detail, which would cause an unexpected narrative turnaround. His father, my granddad, was bedridden with chronic diabetes. The old man was only fifty-two. My father was twenty-two. There were six others below him, five boys and a girl, three in their teens, and the youngest only two. My grandma was a very conservative homebound housewife of early twentieth-century

Ceylon whose knowledge of the world stopped at the gate of Greenlands, the family home set in five acres of blooming tropicana in the heart of Colombo. According to Father, his mother never knew how much property her husband owned, and perhaps, I may add now, how many mistresses he had, installed in each of his coconut estates.

Whenever Father came to the point where he had to mention the condition of his father on the eve of his—Father's—departure to England, he dropped the information with studied casualness. Papa was in bed with a leg amputated. He had chronic diabetes. The lines would drop like a marble into the still clear pool of the narrative. Plop. The sound disturbed like a sudden clap of thunder, and even though we had heard it many times before, we held our breath.

As Father went to bed that night in his room at Greenlands, the last sounds he heard were the voices of his uncles and older male cousins having coffee in the veranda—very much in the English manner—and then he heard the grandfather clock in the dining room strike eleven at night. Those chimes would have dissolved into other imagined sounds as Father roamed the groves of Oxonia in his expectant slumber. But the chimes returned. This time they struck four. He woke up. The lights were on in the house. People were moving around. Voices were agitated. Someone came and stood by his bed.

Artie! Artie!

It was his mother's voice, and she sounded strange. Father knew what she was going to say. He turned around and closed his eyes. Father—his father who was in bed with a leg amputated for diabetes—was dead.

Each time Father narrated this moment in the story something bothered me. How come he could turn away and close his eyes when his father was dead? How come he was so sure his mother was going to tell him that his father was dead? I kept feeling, and the feeling kept getting stronger over the years, that maybe Father always knew he would not be going to England; that deep within him there was a secret inhibition that kept him from going. Why? Now that was part of a gray area I could never clear. The whole aftermath of Father's aborted trip to England is a gray area. Perhaps another story lies hidden there. For the moment I wish to return to that point in my narrative when at the age of sixteen, in a sad little house with dirty peeling walls and smelly cramped spaces in a village eight miles southeast of Colombo, I had secretly opened a set of drawers locked by a single wooden flap in Father's baize-topped writing desk (this desk had been brought down from Greenlands at some point in Father's life when he set up a separate home, and would have been there in his room when Father turned away and closed his eyes as his mother said his father was dead at four o'clock in the morning on a day sometime in 1922 and Father's life took a nosedive) and was going through some documents neatly folded and kept in a metal box of sea-green color that had a now-faded-chrome-plated handle and no lock.

The love letters. Written on ruled paper, neatly folded, and kept in a fair-sized bundle inside the metal box, they came immediately after the letter from Jesus College, Oxford. If discovered and read under different circumstances, I would have hiccupped with laughter. They were sentimental and stupid. The banality of the feelings expressed came more from the language than from the sentiments lying beneath. Father caused irrepressible laughter whenever he spoke his mother tongue, Sinhala. In his love letters, written, obviously to Mother, in Sinhala—because she knew no English—he was caught between two worlds; desire, tightly corseted, almost throttled and whispering hoarsely through Victorian prudery in a language in which the writer was near-illiterate, the result was not hilarious. It was disturbing: Mrs. Henry Wood's *East Lynne* — prescribed reading at Greenlands — in pidgin Sinhala.

All the letters began with a wonderful line: "To my Little Angel." However it wasn't wonderful in Sinhala. The concept of "angel" is alien to the language, it is not in its genes, and there is no corresponding word. What was in currency, at the time those letters were written, especially among the Christians, was a colloquial corruption of the English word. Phonetically in Sinhala it sounds more like a "goblin." Poor Mother. And all the letters were signed: "Asoka" — obviously a pseudonym. Why? Once more the deceit, the deliberate attempt to avoid, to conceal, like in the diary entry of my birth. *Asoka*. First syllables of Arthur and Solomon combined. Clever, even creative. Arthurian legend, biblical myth, and Indian history, all in one. It was no laughing matter. Within me a feeling moved, one octave up on the scale, towards fury.

Beyond the love letters of Asoka and beneath them, on the floor of the metal box, lay the final document, the crucial one. Some vague instinct in my adolescent mind, yet untrained in the ways of the adult world, began tracing a line, connecting certain things together, from as far back as memory began; the sound of the car horn long before it reached the gate creating both wish and fear, the same fear gnawing within as evening came in the sad house where we were poor, the lonely walk through the dark midnight in search of Father when he had walked out of home after a quarrel with Mother, and the anxiety he may have gone forever, before seeing that silhouette at the top of the incline where the roads met, the cold clinical diary entry on the day I was born, the Asoka of the love letters; the line had to end somewhere, giving the whole sequence a head, a reason, and looking at the document that lay at the bottom of the metal box, I knew I had reached the head of a long snake — that was how I felt at that moment, when, at sixteen, I had broken open Father's secret drawers and was looking at the bottom of a metal box in the second drawer.

I unfolded the document.

Long flowing letters handwritten with flourishes and curlicues in now paling black ink filled the sections. It was certainly not Father's handwriting. The paper would have been white in the beginning. Now lying at the bottom of that metal box for years it had acquired the dull off-white of old paper. The folds were sharply creased from being long in that position. The first thing I saw was my name. Then two sections below was my mother's. It filled the entire section in two lines: Rupasingha Arachchige Agnes Tikiri Menike Palipana Rupasingha. Her second name, after the very Caucasian Agnes, and the maternal surname following immediately after, flaunt her highland roots, of which she was intensely proud. My maternal grandmother, once again according to family legend, came down from the hills when she was sixteen. She never went back, and my mother never saw those ancestral hills till she was well past thirty. But those dark brooding Kandyan Mountains lay in her blood, and she bequeathed them to her only son. I am drawn to the tragic highlands of my country by some atavism, and the shrill metal pipes of their ritual beckon me like some long-lost ancestral chord. Mother would have certainly insisted that her full name be included in that declaration of birth of her first-born.

Two cages below was Father's name. He had added an old family name abandoned two generations ago when his ancestors came to the city from the mid-south. Apart from that, nothing seemed odd, until my attention was drawn to the part of the document that inquired if the parents were married. The answer given was "No." From this point on the format of the document was slowly coming into focus. There were two sections between my name and Mother's, which I had skipped over. The first referred to the gender of the one whose birth was being registered, and the next one was for the father. This was blank. But then, in what capacity was Father's name on the document where it was? His name was entered in the "Informant's" section. Arthur Solomon de Fonseka Abeysekara, alias Asoka of those quaint love letters was, as recorded in my birth certificate, not my father, but the "Informant" for the world to know, whenever it becomes necessary, that a child had been born to a woman by the name of Agnes. But then who was its father? Who takes the biological responsibility, if not the legal one?

That moment on that fateful day in that dirty messy cramped little room, as I kept looking at that piece of decaying paper found at the bottom of a green-colored metal box inside the second drawer of a set of drawers in Father's baize-topped writing desk, which was closed by a wooden flap, the lock of which I had opened with a hair pin, many things came together and began to have meaning.

This story begins there. Five years later when Father came into my room late one morning to announce I had become a man, he was only a shadow in my life. The book he presented me was tossed aside. It remained unread and unopened. Five years after I turned twenty-one, I married and left home. Among the books I took away with me J.S.C. Abbott's *Life of Napoleon* wasn't one. One year later, when I began revisiting my parental home, I saw it among the few books Father still had. Of the large collection of books he had when I was a child, less than fifty remained. They were neatly arranged on a single shelf made of cheap boxwood in the room next to the veranda, which Father occupied now.

On an exceptionally cold morning on the first day of October in the year 1988, a friend came home in a taxi. The dark of a long night still remained in pools at six in the morning when he arrived. He worked in a private hospital and had come because that morning the telephone lines weren't working. Father had died half an hour ago. He was admitted to hospital the previous evening. The circumstances were sad, almost tragic.

Mother had passed away more than a year earlier, and Father had moved to a house in a rural suburb of Colombo. My sister, the elder of the two, who remained unmarried at forty and worked as a secretary in a law firm, stayed with him and kept house. The younger girl, having gone through university and become a teacher, had married a colleague and settled in his hometown, far away, on the eastern slopes of the central hills. We saw her only rarely. Since Mother's death, Father hardly spoke. He remembered that the last thing Mother did before she retired to bed the night she died was to iron his shirt, because he had an appointment with the doctor the next morning. He had palpitations and Dr. Jins Attygalle, a relative, was keeping an eye on him. Other than that, he was in good health, for an eighty-eight-year-old man whose last forty years were hard ones. Mother woke—around four in the morning, according to Sister, which must be correct because they slept in the same room—and stood up to find her way in the dark to the toilet. She tottered and fell and the back of her head hit the headboard. Death had been instantaneous. Mercifully. Father remained silent, stone-faced, throughout the funeral ceremony. When the pyre was lit, I saw him getting rather unsteady on his feet. I gave him my hand. He gripped it fiercely, and someone brought a chair. After that he never spoke, unless spoken to, and that too in a very distant manner as if he was in some other zone. We felt he was waiting to join Mother. But the way he died was not the way we had wanted him to go.

When my sister went to work, Father was alone in the house. Each day, before going to work, she would prepare his lunch and lay it carefully on the table. She would tell him not to open the front door for any strangers and she would lock it before she left the house. The key was always with him, though. One day a man came. He had come through the gate, which was unlocked, and tapped at the door. He had a parcel for my sister—the younger of the two, the teacher, living in the hills. Father opened the door. The man wanted a glass of water. He had been searching for the house for a long time, he said, and was very thirsty. It was near high noon. Father went to get the glass of water. When he returned, the man had locked the door and pointed a knife at Father. He then began burgling the house. According to Father, he went up to the man and threw a fist at him, and the man had kicked.

When my sister returned in the evening, she found Father sprawled on the floor. He was conscious and could speak, but could not get up. It was a little past six in the evening and night was falling when my telephone rang.

At the hospital, he was referred to the orthopedic surgeon who said Father's arm was broken. Father wasn't sure where the burglar's kick had connected. But we were relieved that he had escaped with only a broken arm. The surgeon even found it vastly amusing that Father, at eighty-eight, had challenged a burglar with his bare fists. That was until Dr. Jins Attygalle rushed in and found the condition far more complicated. "There's hemorrhage in the intestines. He has been kicked in the stomach," the aging doctor whispered angrily to me. The brothers came, one by one. Only four were alive. The sister and the youngest brother had died. They were all highly successful professionals, now retired. Father was given an injection and a sedative. Dr. Attygalle was noncommittal. He wanted to wait till the following morning. Once he left there was nothing to do. The friend, the one who came in a taxi the next morning, promised to wait on Father. We could go. Father's fourth brother, Uncle Oscar, was still there with me at nine in the night. Once he left, I was alone with Father. He was still wide awake. I kept looking at him. He looked frail and delicate. The face was fair and much younger than his age. Was it the light at an angle on him? Or was it a pallor? I wasn't sure. I thought he wanted to talk to me. But I placed my hand on his forehead, perhaps the very first time I had done something like that where Father was concerned. "Try to sleep," I said, and he smiled faintly. He was curling up, like a little child. May be he was feeling cold. I pulled the white blanket over and around his shoulders. "Are you comfortable?" I asked him, my hand once more on his forehead. He gave me that inscrutable smile again.

We held the funeral at a parlor, because it would be easy for his relatives, most of whom lived in the city. He had many, and he had been in touch with all of them. They loved Uncle Artie. I lived near the city at a place that would have been very convenient for them; Mother's funeral had been in my house. But now my wife was expecting her first child. At thirty-nine I had married for the third time, and ten years later we decided to have a child. My wife could afford that. She was fifteen years my junior. I was one year less than half a century when Father died. Looking back now, I wonder why I didn't feel bad not having the funeral in my house. Perhaps something of the old hurt still lingered, despite that fleeting warmth felt at the hospital.

Father had regularized his marriage in the late seventies.

I was on my second marriage, unhappy and turbulent, when he brought me a copy of the amended birth certificate.

I received it coldly. He must have felt the hostility within me.

"The times were different," he said apologetically. "You must try to understand."

I remained silent for a long time. I felt that if I spoke, all the pent-up anger would explode. I suppose he knew it, and he got up to go. "Let's sit down when you're free one day, just the two of us, and have a frank talk. I want you to know everything." I continued to remain silent.

After Father's death, my sister, who had kept home for him, didn't want to live in that house. It was a rented house and the last one that we, my two sisters and I, could call our parental home. There was nothing to inherit, nothing to go back to, no central place with a reason for family gatherings anymore. Since we never owned property, and always lived in rented homes, the close came easily. Sister was moving into an apartment closer to the city to live on her own. The other sister in the hills had almost become a stranger. The few items of furniture, some of them coming from the days of the big house where the red Jaguar with the long bonnet tooted its horn for me long before it reached the gate, were divided between the two sisters. The writing desk, with the baize lining now completely gone, was still there, and I gave it to my eldest child—a daughter, from my first marriage. The wood flap that closed the drawers was gone. The diaries in the first drawer were still there, but there was no green-colored metal box in the second one. I wonder what had happened to it. Did my sisters ever see that box and the contents inside? Were they deliberately destroyed? If so by whom?

There were very few books, and those were all from Father's belongings that I wanted to take home. Among those books that I packed into a single cardboard box was J.S.C. Abbott's

Life of Napoleon. It had been twenty-eight years then since I first received that book. It still failed to interest me — or was it the association? I threw the book into the box without opening it.

The cardboard box containing the few books Father had left behind remained in a corner of my study, ignored and untouched for nearly a year. One day I began to rearrange the place. I opened the box and took out the books, one by one. I needed space and wanted to get rid of that box. I was certain most of its contents could be thrown away. The first book that came out was a finely illustrated hardcover on King Ludwig of Bavaria. I remembered Father telling me once that if I ever went to Germany, I should go and see the wonderful palaces and castles Ludwig had built all over his kingdom. Then there were some textbooks from his school days. They were mostly on British history, and I remembered Father bringing them over in batches, obviously from the family collection at Greenlands. In one of those books a child had drawn motor cars in a pencil. One car had a long bonnet. That would have been the Jaguar, and the artist would have been me, around age five. The next book that came out of that cardboard box was Abbott's *Life of Napoleon.* I opened it, for the first time. I did so casually with one hand, the other hand holding the book by the spine, and as my thumb flipped the pages, the old and torn jacket separated from the front hard cover. Something fell. It was a folded piece of paper that had been between the jacket and the hard cover. I took time closing the book and placing it on the table by my side, all the time never taking my eyes off the piece of folded paper lying on the ground, like it was a live thing that could escape any moment. I picked it up. It was a small piece of paper folded in quarters. I remembered Asoka's love letters. But this was in English, and the paper wasn't ruled. Father's neat and steady fist had kept perfect lines, one below the other. It was dated *7 May 1960.* The day I became twenty-one. Two spaces below the date came the following wish: *To my most beloved and only son-and-heir with fondest wishes for a peaceful and happy manhood. From your affectionate Father.*

Then came the following quote:

Be and continue poor young man, whilst others around you grow rich by fraud and disloyalty. Be without power or position, whilst others achieve theirs by flattery. Forego the gracious pressure of the hand for which others cringe and crawl. Wrap yourself in your own virtue and seek a friend and thy daily bread. If in your cause, you have gone gray with unbleached honour, bless God and die.
    Heinzelmann.

That's the quote that hangs on my office wall. For me it is a complete portrait of Father with all his contradictions. The subtext contains the tragedy of his life, which I have tried to lay bare here. In a way it is also my story. As I look at it I see Father running through the rain at the news of my birth. Then I ask why the elusive entry in the diary. I hear the Jaguar toot its horn a long way before it reaches the gates of that big house by the fir trees, and I see those quaint love letters at the bottom of that sea-green-colored metal box signed *Asoka*. Then that blank section in my birth certificate, and I ask why? I also see him turn away and close his eyes when his mother tells him his father is dead, and I ask him why he didn't go to England even at a later date. Wasn't there something more than just the responsibility of looking after the family estate and his brothers and the only sister? Was the Little Angel somewhere there even at that time in his life?

    Father, how do I read the contradiction between the life of Napoleon, a story of unbridled ambition, and the prescription for a life of Spartan denial that you slipped under the jacket of that book you gave me when you were sixty and I was twenty-one?

We need to sit down and have that long frank talk, just the two of us. You must tell me everything. I will listen. I have the time now.

END

P.S.
Incidentally, who is Heinzelmann of your quote? I have asked my German friends. They don't seem to know. Even the encyclopedia can't help.

Elsewhere

—

Something Like a Love Story

Everything was elsewhere.

As I stood at the edge of the playground—looking beyond where there was once a strip of paddy and rubber trees on the high ground on the far side, and through which there was a footpath going to a house that I knew was there but had never seen—and where the paddy field was and the rubber trees stood, all I could see now were rooftops with the antennae sticking like twigs—my mind was elsewhere.

Behind me was the playground looking much smaller than I remembered—and on the edge of that other side where the ground sloped down to the hostel was the olive tree, not the olives of Greece and Italy, but sour little fruits, oval in shape with a thin layer of green flesh covering a spiked seed, and the flowers, white and in tassels, that had the smell of semen, and as boys, when we passed the tree, looked at each other furtively, in secret communion, guilty, and then looked at the girls who kept looking down—and now my mind was elsewhere again.

I am six months before fifteen, and it is a day in January—late morning—and it is the first day of the first term in that school. It is also my first day there having come from somewhere else, and I am walking down the concrete steps going from the pavilion to the playground that looks huge to me. It's PT time, just before the interval, and the ground is filling up with boys and girls forming into squads—moving pieces of white—and watching them my heart beats faster like it does when I am expecting something to happen.

The sun is warm, not hot like it is at other times, because it is January and still not midday, and it is pleasant to have the sun on your face. Within me I also feel like this is the beginning of something. Perhaps it is all the girls down there — so many of them — in crisp white uniforms glowing in the clear light. In the school that I had left to come here there were no girls.

When the drills begin I cannot take my eyes off the girls as they skip; hands up, hands down, legs out, legs in; hems go up, thighs flash, white uniforms stretch and little breasts press against the starched cloth; slowly the air becomes heavy with the warm smell of sweating bodies; it is good to feel the sun pouring over you, and the breeze creeping around you stealthily like a cat; it keeps low, hugging the ground, caressing the legs, because we are up on a land surrounded by paddy fields on three sides, the low-moving breeze rises up from there, and brings with it the smell of mud and sun-warmed water of ripening paddy and something else that I know is the smell of rubber, leaves both new and old, on the trees and on the ground, fresh and decaying, dry and damp, of freshly oozing latex dripping along the panels cut almost at the break of day. But there is something else waiting for me this first morning on my first day at this school where there are girls drilling in the warm sun, perspiring slowly in their starched white uniforms.

A bell rings, we break formation and begin walking out of the sun-drenched ground, chattering loud and wild in delightful chaos and disarray. Very few walk up the steps to go through the pavilion, like the way I came. The movement is towards a point where the school compound slopes down to meet the level of the playground and where there is a narrow entry point to the higher plane where the school buildings are. It is natural, I think, to go through there, because we are tired after all that hands-up-hands-down-legs-out-legs-in business to climb steps; fair enough; but that's where the olive tree is, and today it is festooned with those flowers like white tassels.

There were two water taps here, and the girls and boys stopped almost by habit; they clustered round the taps, not so much drinking but screaming and splashing each other with water; the smell of sweat and of sun-warmed bodies mingled with the guilt-laden scent of olive flowers; it weaved some kind of spell and held the children swarming round the taps like the pack-sense of animals.

I wasn't thirsty, but I stood, held in that collective feeling, and then I saw her. It was a face, wet with water and sweat, strands of loose hair streaking it, and two eyes that looked away and then returned to lock me in a briefly held gaze.

Fifteen years later, the same eyes look at me through the midday glare, the dust, and the heat of the Pettah Central Bus Stand. Now she is in sari, heavy round the hips, fuller every-where. Many things have happened since the scent of olive flowers mingled with the body heat and held us in some vaguely felt something. Now it is the heat of high noon falling from the sky and rising like vapor from the asphalt, mingling with the smell of rotting fruit, of garbage, and of sweat-soaked bod-ies. But the eyes are unchanged, looking at me from across many gone years with that warm glow and promise of forbid-den things.

Once more it is elsewhere. I come back and it is in the beginning.

But it is a little after—a month, few weeks, or perhaps a lit-tle more than a month, I am not sure—that moment at the tap under the olive tree, and the sinful scent of those flowers hang-ing like white tassels from the branches and strewn on the ground. Her hands are wrapped, coiled around my neck, and my knees hurt, perhaps they are bleeding from pressing against the bare ground on the slope where the grass is thin on the hard red gravelly earth. I am wet, and I feel the wet on her, and that sinful scent has exploded and lay all over; but we are not under the olive tree, because the sun, red and big, is going down over the paddy and the tops of rubber trees are as if they are on fire, and this is not the view from where the olive tree is.

Now the rubber trees are gone, and I see the antennae like dead men's hands. No green paddy, no red sun. Everything looks pale and cadaverous. But I feel the scent, and now it is all around me, taking me back once more to elsewhere.

If this has to have a beginning, it began at the water taps at the edge of the playground under the olive tree with flowers that smelled of sin on my first day at this school where there were boys and girls, and when I was six months less than fifteen, and when two eyes on a face wet with sweat and water and streaked with strands of hair looked at me like no one else had looked; or so I felt, and was sure, as I kept thinking all day and all night.

It was all there was to think about, as the lessons in the classroom droned away vaguely somewhere and the open page on the desk a vague blur and a reedy voice was reciting something; *A step more light a step ... true ... heath flower ... its dew*, and then something about *Relative velocity of trains crossing each other in opposite directions* and then *double drawbridge cannon musket fire and smoke, what Madame Defarge was doing and what Jerry Cruncher was doing*, and through all that, big dark eyes on a wet face, kept looking, *Geographical Discoveries, Vasco da Gama sailing round the Cape of Good Hope, Yes, you! Who was the Sun King?* The two eyes and the wet face vanish, and the mind is a blank, but the big eyes are somewhere there in the blank poised to reappear.

At the tuck shop, Lionel, the big bully of the class, but who for some reason has become my friend, slaps me hard on my back.

What's up?

What do you mean, what's up?

Between you and that one?

Which one?

We call her *That One,* but sometimes we call her Jane.

Why Jane?

Oh, that's from the Tarzan comics. Jane is Tarzan's girl-friend. She lives in the jungle. We called this one *Jungle* 'cos she came from *Out There.*

Lionel points his hand vaguely towards somewhere beyond the edge of the playground, where the land slopes down to the paddy and then rises up to the dark rubber woods.

Then we called her *Jane* because in the Tarzan comics Jane lives in the jungle.

Silence.

Then Lionel speaks again, and he sounds serious.

You are one of us now. We like you, and wouldn't like to see you in trouble.

I listen, and Lionel keeps talking. We are walking away from the tuck shop, not to our class but towards the music room. Out there it is quiet and deserted at this time. Seated on a bench under one of the wide-canopied araliya trees, which are in permanent white-bloom, Lionel tells me many things about *That One.*

She is common property. Most of the boys have legged her (that is when a boy inserts his dick between a girl's thighs and keeps pushing it back and forth until he comes, which they let you do because it is safe). If anyone gets serious with her, he becomes a joke, an outcaste, because she is more than just a fast one. She is crazy. She comes from a foul background. Her mother is a tart who is now being kept by a rich man. The father is dead; they say the mother and that rich man got together and killed him. Now they say the man is keeping both mother and daughter. He is a powerful man who comes in a big car.

Go on.

Lionel slapped me hard as the bell rang, and we got up to go.

But don't get serious. Don't let her get serious either. She tries hard to.

It was obvious Lionel too has legged her.

In the next days the eyes kept looking, and I didn't look away either, but I was careful not to let others see I was looking, until one day we walked into each other in a corridor where we were the only ones at that moment. We both stopped like we had been waiting for this. We kept looking at each other, and I thought she had an unusual face, like she was not one of us; a complexion that wasn't fair but not dark either; it was slightly yellow, a tinge of the Far East, and her hair had a slight copper glow.

I did not know what to say, but couldn't keep staring either. Her eyes made me nervous; I thought they didn't blink, and I spoke because the silence was frightening.

What's your name?

The lips opened and remained like they were expecting something, and then a sound came; not a giggle, but a laugh held back somewhere.

Didn't they tell you? The first thing anyone learns here is my name. Jane. Tarzan's mate. But that's not my name.

What's it then?

It's a dirty word. They don't say it loud here.

What could I say other than gape stupidly. It was she who spoke again.

You'll know it soon. That's if you really want to know. There's a price on it.

It didn't take too long.

But there were other things I came to know.

She was the basketball star of the school. The finest shooter ever in this school. I saw her in action. Leaping like a swift mare, thighs flashing, and the ball dropping through the net like it was the most natural thing to happen. She was also the fastest thing on two legs in a skirt; or so they said. Wait till the sports meet. That was another six months away.

That's why they cannot send her home. There are other reasons too.

There are some male staff members who had crossed the strip of paddy, and gone through the dark rubber trees *Out There*. In the night.

What for? (This was stupid me.)

To pray. You stupid. (This was Lionel.)

For the mother?

Maybe for both. We are still trying to find out.

There were other things I saw. The girls avoided her. It was funny the way they fell silent and looked at each other, or how they cocked up their heads, stiffened their backs, hissed under their breath as Jane walked up or passed by. It was also funny to note how Jane walked, looking over and through them, swinging her hips deliberately to say, *Look at me you little bitches, look at me and eat your tongues, stare until your wicked eyeballs jump out of their sockets, run round and round and round like a head-chopped-off chicken and drop dead in your stinking blood.*

She is bad, one would say.

Bad? She is evil, says another.

I think she has an evil disease, says the third.

Let's go men, they all say together.

The teachers, both male and female, loved her; they couldn't do without her. She was constantly running errands for them; bringing things for them; half-ripe-sour-green mangoes when female teachers were pregnant, juicy honey-laden waraka and divul, thick kolikuttu and seedless rambutan when the teachers were either not pregnant, had stopped getting pregnant, or had never gotten pregnant. There were other tributes for the male teachers: kotala himbutu (an herb) for Kimbula (The Crocodile), the prefect of discipline, because he had chronic diabetes; a special kind of oil Jane's mother prepared at home from king coconut spiced with cinnamon for Mudda, the hostel warden with a fierce mustache who had catarrh—he was one of those suspected of having crossed the paddy field and walked through the rubber land in the night; freshly plucked green-green strong-tasting betel leaves with areca nut for Patholaya (Snake Gourd), the six-foot-tall thin-as-a-beanstalk mathematics teacher who chewed betel all day long; bees' honey, the real stuff (because Jane's maternal uncle was somewhere in Mahiyangana, where the indigenous people who collect the pure bees' honey from inaccessible rock crevices live), for Pina (the principal), who was nearing sixty but dyed his hair and—it was whispered—applied Pond's Vanishing Cream to look young, and who put his arm round girls' shoulders whenever he spoke to them.

Boys took her for granted; she was the stray puppy everyone could play with or kick as they pleased, the mongrel permanently at the door, never taken inside. Each one of them had their turn petting her secretly; never going beyond for pain of being permanently ostracized by the boys' own fraternity, and worse, to be shunned like a leper by the girls, the clean ones, the legitimate ones, the ones to be wooed and won through sheer hard work and persistence.

That was the convention, the unwritten yet sacred rule, inviolate.

Was it this taboo that made her so attractive to me, or was it simply her legendary largesse with those illicit favors? Despite all the brainwashing by Lionel, and by a growing circle of friends—I was fast becoming popular—I felt myself going over the top, flipping over, doomed. Jane was everywhere within me, eyes wide open, thighs flashing, hips shaking, at all times of the day, and in the night too when I would wake up wet and alarmed with guilt.

I come back.

The day is dying over the dead paddy field, and the TV antennae are fading against the slowly darkening sky, but in my mind everything is bathed in a golden light; it lay in pools on the green paddy, and it drips down the rubber trees; I hear the song of homing birds; is it now or then? Must be then, and I get that heavy scent of olive flowers all over me and her as we lay on the thin grass covering the hard red earth, my knees hurting, and I am sinfully wet. Towards the far end of the little valley, between the high ground where I stand and the rubber trees on the other side, the sun is going behind the faint line of trees.

Lionel and Suren are up somewhere on the playground, keeping watch for us; I can't see them; they were to blow a whistle if someone was to come this way; up there many were practicing for the forthcoming sports meet; the whistle never blew.

She was already up. Her eyes went up to the edge of the playground; voices floated down from up there. The head lowered slowly, and the eyes looked at me. I saw something different there, something soft gentle and sad. I watched her going down the slope, disappearing behind a thick hedge and reappearing on the paddy field, moving along a thin ridge separating the paddy plots, blending into the dark under the rubber trees. She didn't look back even once. Daylight lingered on the treetops. Down below I could still see the sky's reflection on the pools of water. But the glow was gone.

Suren appeared on the edge sharp against the sky, and then came Lionel. They stood there, and Lionel made a signal. As agreed, I was not to come up, but was to keep moving along the lower level through the bush and reach the quadrangle in the middle school, and then up the stone steps going behind the shrine room to surface near the tuck shop. I walked slowly. I was not happy. Something was bothering me. It was not the feeling you had when you cheated on your parents, or did something you were not supposed to do. It was like I had hurt someone who should not be hurt. It had something to do with that look in her eyes before she left, and then the way she walked down the slope and across the paddy field all the way to disappear in the dark under those rubber trees.

When I came to the tuck shop, Lionel and Suren were already there. Those who had come for athletics were leaving, singly or in groups. They came lazily along the drive that ran along the main building all the way to the gate. The tuck shop was before you came to the gate. Those who were going had to pass the tuck shop. Some stopped to have a drink. Those who already knew me looked surprised.

Didn't see you at the grounds, said some, and Lionel kicked me under the table where we were seated.

Don't say anything. Just grin.

I grinned.

They looked puzzled and went away, and it was Suren who kicked me gently, this time.

How did it go?

I grinned.

You don't look happy. That was Lionel.

You messed up, right? That was Suren.

No, I said grinning again.

Don't con. It was the first time, right?

I said nothing. I did not want to say it was my first time with a girl.

Don't worry chum. We all mess up first time. You'll be right soon. Get her to teach you how. That's how we learned.

Where I stood now, the light was paling. I had planned to

walk along the old path where I walked once-upon-a-time, through the bushes and across the quadrangle and up the stone steps behind the shrine room all the way to the tuck shop after I lay with her under the bush on the slope on the thin grass on the hard red earth and as the evening lay glowing on the paddy field and poured all over the rubber trees, and the sun was a ball of fire at the end of the slender valley.

That was thirty-six years ago.

Today, the sun was anemic, and there was no paddy field across which she walked, never even once looking back, and no rubber trees under which it was dark where she disappeared. I could not have gone through that memory path to the tuck shop as I had wanted to, because the quadrangle was enclosed by another building, and perhaps the stone steps behind the shrine room were gone, too. Only the tuck shop remained where it was. But it had changed shape, and today being Saturday, it was closed when I drove in through the gate.

I went back over the years and walked out of the tuck shop on that fading day with Lionel and Suren, and there were still a few boys walking towards the gate after sports practice, but we went the other way, behind the tuck shop through a footpath to the country road that went away from the High Level Road, because Lionel lived on this road, and we wanted to walk him home, and after doing that Suren and I walked back to the High Level Road through another byway, and Suren stood with me until the bus came to take me home, and I remember hoping that the bus would never come, because I did not want to go home, because for some reason I was feeling quite low. I just wanted to keep walking until something that was bothering me inside would go away. But I went home, because for a boy not yet fifteen there was nowhere else to go when night was falling.

I remember I couldn't sleep. Each time sleep came I would

see her walking across the thin strip of paddy, the day's dying glow around her, a lonely animal going somewhere, someplace it didn't want to be. There was a swelling within me that pressed against my chest like the rib cage was going to burst and I would get up in alarm. When that pressure subsided, the scent of olive flowers filled the room, and I wanted to be with her just like the way we were on that thin grass over the hard red earth. I reached for my knees where it was still raw with that pressing against the ground. Then I imagined her body against mine, warm, exuding olive-flower scent, and sleep kept coming like something very pleasant spreading itself over me. The golden twilight, the white-clad girl crossing the field, moving into the dark under the rubber trees, her white school uniform holding itself against the dark almost like a slowly dissolving phantom, until the pressure began to build up within me, all over again, pulling me out of that dream violently; over and over again it went like a looped movie, until in the early hours of dawn when the first birds began to sing I found myself crying. I cried hard, silently, into the pillow. Trying to muffle the sound for my parents in the next room not to hear, my chest began to burn.

Lying exhausted, face pressed into the pillow, I began to recount the minutiae of that moment—maybe it was only five minutes, but time was stretched like in slow motion—the dying fall of the climax. There was a line repeated in my ear, heard vaguely like it was coming from afar, almost the plaintive cry of a wounded bird.

I can't go home. Don't let me go home.

Perhaps it was this plea echoed in my mind later, much clearer than when it was first whispered, that made me cry. There was a feeling of helplessness within me, a painful realization of my inadequacy. It was more self-pity than anything else, I think, in retrospect.

The next few months were hard for me; hard to hold back from being sucked into a whirlpool of calf-love; harder to keep my growing circle of possessive friends from knowing the extent of my involvement.

Don't let me go home.

That was the key to the world across the paddy field and in the dark under the rubber trees; it was a refrain, and like the dark, it frightened me and pulled me to it all at once; it caused an emotional vertigo; I was terrified of falling and longing to fall at the same time. Or so I think, now.

The olive-flower scent possessed us; the moments in which it exploded like a mysterious choking fragrance became more, and with each moment I came away numbed with some new knowledge about the world across the paddy field and in the dark beyond the rubber trees.

Last night he came to me.

Why didn't you tell Mother?

Mother? She is more scared of him than me.

There was another time I found welts on her back.

What happened?

He beat me.

That was another night I couldn't sleep because I kept see-ing her screaming in pain, and kept waking up, and when the first birds of dawn started singing, I was crying; crying not for her but for me. I wanted to walk across that paddy field in the night, move stealthily like a leopard, lay in wait, and kill that man. There was a kukri knife at home, something an uncle had brought from the war and had given my father; it was hanging on the wall; I wanted to steal it, but it was big, and for days I kept planning the act; I would slice the man's throat, and watch him choke in his own blood, dying slowly like a chopped-up monster. Even when I was planning I knew I couldn't do it;

it was way beyond me; when I came to terms with my pathetic condition, I cried again.

Last night I saw my father in a dream.

He looked beautiful. Like the last time I saw him.

Earlier, one day when we were lying somewhere on that slope beyond the edge of the playground overlooking the paddy field, she had told me of her father, how he was the most wonderful person in her life as a child, how she loved to sleep cuddled in his arms, even long after she ceased to be a baby, and how he carried her everywhere. He was a beautiful father, she said.

Fathers can't be beautiful, they are men, and men cannot be beautiful, only women are, I said. (I avoided saying anything about mothers, because I knew she hated her mother.)

But my father was beautiful, she insisted.

The day he kissed me and went, promising to bring me a box of crayons, because I liked to draw, and I walked with him up to the gate, and stood there, and he kept turning round and waving at me until he took that bend and disappeared, never to come again, he looked more beautiful than I had ever seen him.

Why didn't he come back? I had asked.

I am still trying to find out, she had said.

What do the others say?

Which others?

Your mother, for instance.

Oh, she! She says he had gone away from the country. But I don't believe her. I think they did something to my father.

Who did?

My mother and that man.

Which man?

That man my mother is with. I'll kill him one day.

I had to close her mouth to stop her from screaming, and she dug her teeth ferociously into the flesh of my palm over her mouth, and it hurt through the night, and I had to tell a great big lie when I got home.

Now she is with me once again and telling me her beautiful father came to her in a dream.

He kept saying something, but no sound came from the mouth; only the lips kept forming words. We were somewhere in a dark wood, and he began walking backwards, away from me, and I wanted to run towards him, to stop him from going away, but I couldn't run, and I wanted to scream, wanting him not to go away, but I couldn't scream, it was like I was choked with sand.

Then came the chorus line.

Don't let me go home. I can't go home.

Now it's now once again, and I am still on the edge of the play-ground looking down the slope—cleared of the bush where I lay with her once-upon-a-time with the scent of olive flowers all around us—towards where once there was a paddy field, and beyond that to where there were rubber trees with a per-manent dark under them, and now all that gone, and I can-not walk on that path that lay through the quadrangle of the middle school because there is a new building that blocks that path moving along my memory, up a flight of stone steps—which may not be there now—to surface near the tuck shop, to meet Lionel and Suren who are waiting for me, to find out how it went.

The night seems near, but the anemic light in the sky and on the ground refuses to die, and once again I am elsewhere.

Two eyes looking through the noonday glare, the dust, and the body heat of sweating crowds, the smell of rotting fruit and vegetables and diesel fumes. Pettah Central Bus Stand. I see her after twelve years. I had stopped seeing those eyes looking at me, and it was like the first moment of contact near the two water taps under the olive tree. Now I am in the middle of the road, horns blaring, buses belching filthy smoke, people rushing pushing running shoving in a nonstop motion, and she is walking calmly with measured steps towards me (this is the one image of her etched in my mind still and will always be, because in this image I see her entire self and her story I am trying to relate at length).

When she stops she is very close to me. I am twenty-six years old, but my heart begins to pound, and I am almost certain she can hear it. She is calm, the fire is gone from her eyes, and there is a gentle glow there, and a softness of lines all about her, and I begin to wonder whether it is the sari she is wearing—a sheen of mauve sprayed with delicate white blossoms, a darker-shaded pallu loosely thrown around the shoulders making her look as a woman in full bloom.

Hello is all I can say.

Do you remember me? That's what she says, and those eyes with the fire doused and with a gentle glow, smile. Yes, it was the eyes that smiled.

Why not?

It's been a long time.

Now the smile evaporates from the eyes; but the glow remains. I remembered the sad twilight that lay on the paddy field she crossed alone to that dark under the rubber trees where she didn't want to go after we lay for the first time on that slope at the edge of the playground.

We keep looking; it is a difficult place to stand without being swept away by the swirling action around, in the middle of all the traffic.

Let's move over.

She takes my hand and crosses over to the edge of the road and moves between two hawkers to the sidewalk. Even there it is difficult to stand, but at least natural to be looking at each other in silence.

She still holds my hand as if it is the most natural thing, but I feel uncomfortable. Many things have happened since I last saw her twelve years ago.

I dropped out of high school, gate-crashed into marriage, and was now living precariously on the meager earnings of free-lance journalism.

Perhaps she felt my discomfort and released my hand, and there was something like mischief and amusement in those gently glowing eyes.

She spoke first.

I heard you got married?

I grinned and said, Yes.

I hear she is a movie star?

I simply nodded unenthusiastically. The thrill of running away with a movie star in the middle of a film, bringing production to a halt and seeing my name in the papers had palled, and I had realized within weeks that the whole thing was a ghastly misadventure. But there was no going back; my wife was pregnant, and I was supremely miserable.

How are you? I wanted to change the subject.

I am all right.

You must be married? She looked married, and there was a ring on her finger.

Who would marry me?

Why?

She smiled with her eyes again, and I noticed the sadness in them like the dying light across the paddy field.

You know all about me. And still you ask me that question.

There was a complaint in her voice, but no bitterness. It remained gentle and calm.

Where are you going now?

Not that I wanted to know seriously, but it was important to prevent going back to certain things. I had left all that behind me, but now a fear began creeping up like a chill along the spine, the fear of a relapse to some fatal condition that may be lying dormant within me. I couldn't afford that.

She had come to the Kachcheri. Now she was taking the train back home. She was taking the Little Train. That was what people called the train that plied the narrow gauge along the Kelani Valley. Our school was somewhere on that line, and she told me the little railroad town where she lived now; it was way beyond the town of our school, where she lived when we knew each other.

Would you mind walking with me to the station? We could talk then. There is time for my train.

I walked with her, and before I could say anything, she bought me a platform ticket, and we walked slowly along the first platform, climbed steps to an overhead bridge, came down on the far platform, and sat on a passenger bench. The platform was empty, and I felt relaxed for the first time since meeting her.

Where is Subhadra?

Who?

For a moment I could not remember.

The one you went steady with?

Oh, that one. She left school before me. Haven't seen her since.

I remembered now, but only parts of her, and those parts didn't quite reassemble in my memory. She was considered the most glamorous and arrogant girl in school; she played the piano at assembly, sang "Que Sera Sera" like a nightingale, spoke English fluently—this immediately made her someone very special in a school where, although the medium of instruction was English, few were comfortably at home with it—and came to school in a car. She had come from some fancy girls school in Kandy; we named her "Lucie Manette" after the character in Dickens's *A Tale of Two Cities*—our prescribed text for the senior form. All the boys gazed at Subhadra, and she looked at no one; there was no Charles Darnay—the character in Dickens's book who had won Lucie's heart—who stood up to her level, or rather we thought she thought so.

One day I had recited "A Slave's Dream" by Longfellow in the English class. Those days I had been constantly checked in my recitation or prose reading for being too fast; I would begin well, in a measured tone, but was soon going like a runaway train. "Developing horsepower," my English teacher would say; "Stop!" or "Go easy," he would say. But on that day, with Longfellow's poem, I had broken through my manner, and I felt I had found the trick of controlling my voice, pacing it and going along easily. I was conscious of Lucie Manette's presence just one row away at an angle from where I could see her perfectly sculptured profile from the corner of my eye. I was performing for her, my voice dancing like a full-plumed peacock.

As I sat down, Lucie Manette's sculptured profile turned ever so slightly, and on that usually cold and marble face there appeared a smile. My heart leapt like an excited colt; Suren kicked me under the desk.

For the next few days I floated.

For my friends I had become a hero.

I had conquered.

The smiling with each other continued for a few days from a distance. Once more there was the feeling of vertigo; I was dying to cross that space, but it was better to hang on to that smile and only think of all that lay beyond, as the risk of crossing was too terrifying, because I was simply not what I appeared in school.

I was from an impoverished home. We were living on the charity of well-to-do relatives; I had only two shirts and two trousers, and most of the time I wore shoes thrown away by my affluent cousins. I exuded no scent of Old Spice, wore no Arrow shirts with those fancy stiff collars, had no money to buy Cadbury's, the mandatory token of love for your girlfriend. These were the standards set by the hostellers who came from affluent families, whose parents came in cars to fetch them for the weekends and holidays.

But I was the great pretender.

I had created a mythology of myself in which I was born in England. My parents came back to this country when I was seven, and for the next three years I was given private lessons at home. I had to be put through a crash course in my mother tongue—I never credited my poor mother, who taught me Sinhala between her many hours of worry to keep the family going—before I resumed my education here. I was sent to this school because the principal was my father's classmate—which was true—and he wanted me in his school. I may have made it sound almost like the principal thought it was a great big privilege for him to have me in this provincial school.

This entire myth was gift-wrapped in my unusual skill with the English language; teachers looked confused like they heard a crow not caw but sing when I spoke in English. Schoolmates gaped unbelievingly when I read, and more than once, when I wrote an essay, I was cross-examined severely by deeply suspecting teachers to check whether I knew what I had written, or the meaning of some of the words I had used.

The English language was my camouflage, my defense mechanism; it was my Old Spice, my Arrow shirt with the arrogant stiff collar, my bar of Cadbury's chocolate.

With its magic wand, I had made a sphinx smile.

But immediately after I was gripped with fear. This was going to be my moment of reckoning; I had deftly maintained a myth, manipulated to avoid taking my friends home to the sad little house with dirty peeling walls and leaking roof. I had managed cleverly to look smart without satin drill trousers and immaculate white shirts and shining shoes, and with no money, and no parents coming for the prize-giving or the sports meet in a car.

With Lucie Manette, who looked at no boy, suddenly smiling with me, and the body language between us sending the right signals, it would just be a matter of time before we started "carrying on," and then it would be impossible to maintain the myth without inventing more myths until the whole thing exploded in humiliation and shame. But like it was with the eyes that looked at me at the two water taps under the olive tree, I was once again pulled by some irresistible force.

Did you have anything to do with that slut?

That was Lucie Manette, the very first time we went beyond that smile. We were somewhere on the steps leading to the pavilion up from the playground. She had avoided going through the spot near the water taps under the olive tree with the white flowers carrying the smell of semen where the high ground met the playground level, and began going up the steps after drill, stopped, halfway turned round, and smiled. It was almost a command: *Here I am. Walk up, boy, if you have the courage.* She stood there like a reigning queen in spotless white, glistening in the blinding late-morning light. I walked up the steps, and as I was about to reach her, she kept walking ahead of me. Walking through the fixed wood benches on the pavilion, she stopped once again and placed a hand on the backrest of one seat; I looked at the hand, which held a pure white handkerchief in delicate fingers; the skin looked ivory. I raised my eyes, and she looked vaguely amused, but soon her eyes steeled, and there was a pitiless arrogance there.

It was then she fired the question, looking straight at me.

Which one are you talking about?

The one who comes from *out there.*

She pointed her hand vaguely beyond the edge of the playground where the paddy field was; from the high ground where the pavilion was and where we stood, the paddy field could be seen. It was to my back and she faced it, but she avoided looking there, like it was improper or beneath her dignity.

I had to say no, and *no* I said.

Those steely eyes held me, and I held them in mine like it would be fatal to look away; it was the fear of the mongoose facing a cobra.

I hope you are telling me the truth.

Why should I lie?

It was only a half-truth, because her first question was in the past tense. My trysts in the bush on the slope *over there* with the scent of olive flowers exploding around, and in certain other secret corners—never in the open, even when the scent of olive flowers were not around—had stopped as abruptly as they began. Two thugs had accosted me on the lonely country road as I was walking home after cadet training one day, when it was already dark, and held me by my shoulders, one of them on each side, and questioned me about my "connection" with "Grace Nona's Girl," which was how they referred to *Jane,* and promised very seriously to cut my penis and have it stuffed in my mouth if I did not stop fooling around with this girl. The agony of this corporal punishment was going to be further intensified by buggering me continuously until my ass split and

I died purging buckets of blood. All this sounded blood-curdling when expressed in the phonetics of my beloved Sinhala language. I walked home like a zombie, and despite the pleas of my mother to eat something, I fell on the bed and within minutes was burning with high fever, followed by three days of intense purging.

I returned to school one week later with the parental letter requesting that I be excused from all out-of-classroom activities for some time, and that suited me fine, because if I didn't go for PT to the playground, it would be easier to avoid "Grace Nona's Girl." I hardly went out of the classroom, avoided looking towards her class that was on a lower terrace in a direct line downwards if I stood up from my classroom desk and looked through the chicken-coop wire net screening the upper-half of our block. I hardly stood up in those critical days, and if I did, it was only to answer a teacher, and I was careful not to look that way; I knew there would be two cat eyes focused my way from down there, and it would be fatal if I came into its line of sight. Even during PT time I sat hunched at my desk by the wall when the entire school had poured out into the playground. My powerful and loyal friends, especially Lionel and Suren, were most concerned and brought me things from the tuck shop during the interval, and there were times when I thought I saw a peculiar glint in their eyes like they knew. But how could they? It was perhaps my imagination activated by a gnawing fear. Yet I couldn't quite explain why these tough friends of mine encouraged me to remain in seclusion when under normal circumstances they would have tortured a boy for such withdrawals just because he has had a bout of fever and three days of what was called "loose motions." It was not "manly." It was being a "sissy." But why did they mollycoddle me? It was puzzling, yet I felt safe and protected like being at home.

I had avoided visiting that tree at the edge of the vast school compound in a particularly woody area where in a hollow in the massive trunk we had by covenant deposited our letters to each other twice a week. There were times when those letters were deposited every day, and our visits to the tree, separately, became a daily ritual. We lived dangerously alternating between "visits to the tree" and lying on "the thin grass of the slope" overlooking the slender strip of paddy, which turned from translucent green to gold and then to stubble, reflecting the red of the dying day, then turning green once more. The last time we lay there—that was before the two thugs threatened to castrate me—the harvest had been gathered and the red sunlight was reflected like pools of blood in the patches of water on the stubble field.

And now I was in hiding like a frightened mouse.

Three weeks after I had stopped looking through the chicken-coop wire netting and sat huddled in my class and stopped going to "the tree," which also followed that I did not lay in the "thin grass on the slope" with the scent of olive flowers all around, something terrifying happened.

I was in class during PT time, and with everyone out on the playground, there was an awesome silence. I had buried my face in my arms on the desk, feeling wretched, when I heard soft footfalls. They were coming along the long outer veranda, which lay on the sides of our block. I couldn't see because of the half wall, and I was seated. I stood up slowly. *That One* was moving along the narrow space, coming this way. A bright shaft of late morning sunlight lay across her path; her white uniform flashed as she crossed that beam, and her face almost disappeared in the contrast between light and shadow. A ghost on a dark night couldn't have terrified me more.

I ran.

Out of the class, across the netball court with the sun all

over it, into the hall and along its full length, through the narrow exit at the far end into the bio-science lab and between the glass bottles with embalmed snakes and other creatures standing on tables, down the spiraling steps leading to the pathway going towards the hostel, and halfway down that path, the playground came into view, and I saw all that "hands-up—hands-down" business was over and everyone was milling round the two taps under the olive tree, and I took a complete about-turn, running in the opposite direction along the tarred path all the way and ended up at the back of the tuck shop panting and shaking like a hunted deer when Hendrick the tuck shop man saw me, and looking very suspicious said, Now what have you done? And I was too sick to answer, and he looked more suspicious.

I remember still how you ran when I came to see you. I still don't know why.

She giggled, and still holding me in that soft gentle glow in her eyes let out a peal of laughter, and a porter pushing a trolley along the platform looked at us sharply. A train whistled behind us, and I looked back.

No, that is not my train, she said, and I felt unrelieved.

She went back to her story.

The day you ran, I went to the tree and collected all my letters, which lay uncollected for three weeks. I had deposited a letter each day there.

She was recounting all this like it was something very funny.

I couldn't possibly leave them there, because I knew when you ran that it was the end. There was an old well on my way home in the middle of that rubber land, and I dropped the entire bundle into it. I couldn't possibly take them home either.

She laughed again. There were a few passengers now waiting for the train, and when she laughed, they looked at us like we were doing something wrong. I was feeling uncomfortable.

She placed her hand gently on mine. There was no guile in the gesture, and her voice was totally unaffected.

Why did you run?

I could never have told her why, even now. It would have been wrong if I told her the truth. If it was what I believed at the time I ran, I could have told her everything now, perhaps with the same detached amusement with which she was speaking about the past. But there were others whose memory I had to respect.

Six months after I ran, I attended my first school cadet camp and Lionel was in the same platoon. It was my first time and Lionel's third. He was the lance sergeant. The train traveled through the night, taking us up into the hills, and it was getting colder by the hour. The teachers-in-charge traveled first class, and those carriages were far away from ours, with no connecting passages, and we were pretty much to ourselves, free to indulge in forbidden pleasures. The more seasoned among us had brought packets of cigarettes and bottles of liquor buried deep inside trunks. I had never taken alcohol till then, smoked only once, and hadn't liked it because the fumes went down the throat and up somewhere into my head, and I thought I was going to die. But on this journey through the night up into the hills on a slow-moving train taking me on my first cadet camp, I was with Lionel and some of the toughest and knowing boys, not only of my own platoon, but also boys from the other two Colombo schools that constituted our company. Close to midnight, when the "sissies" were dropping into sleep one by one, and the mad screaming and shouting and singing and clapping and beating time on the wooden train doors and on anything else around which made a sound when thumped on had subsided, and only the monotonous rhythm of the train wheels "dlug-dlugging" over the iron rails remained, the "bad ones" got together, and the cigarettes came out, and the bottles were opened. By the early hours of dawn, with frost whitening the closed panes of the train windows, eighteen of us had got roaring drunk on two bottles of coconut arrack. Most of us were acting drunk—over-lisping, over-gesticulating, over-pitching voices—over-everything in a frantic effort to be macho. Only Lionel was genuinely drunk. Somehow I felt that way because he had fallen silent, and there was a glazed look in his eyes; slumped on the train floor, and leaning against a wooden seat, he was frozen in a funny pose. One by one the boys were getting up and moving away as if remembering suddenly they were not drunk; they looked perfectly normal. I remained because Lionel continued to be frozen. I was getting a little concerned because daybreak was near, and within the next two hours we would reach the hill station, and by that time we should be ready for the muster parade on the station platform in the freezing cold. The train had picked up speed as if it had reached its last lap and was breaking into a dash. I kept shaking my friend, and slowly he began to thaw; a hand moved in slow motion and the legs unfolded; he straightened his spine, looked around the compartment littered with sleeping cadets, like dead soldiers after a battle, kept looking at me for some time and smiled, and I was relieved. He asked me whether there were any cigarettes left, and then reached for a half-smoked crumpled fag lying under a seat and began fumbling in his trouser pockets for a match. I had a box in my pocket. I watched him light the cigarette like a seasoned smoker—which he was, at sixteen—and I was full of admiration; he was already my role model.

I want to tell you something before the sun comes up in the morning.

Lionel sounded strange, almost like an elderly man speaking to a boy. And what he told me in that voice with the train wheels clashing in a monotonous rhythm beneath us and the compartment rocking us like we were in a cradle, was that those two thugs who threatened to chop my manhood if I didn't stop fooling around with "Grace Nona's Girl" were stage-managed by him and Suren. One was Suren's sister's servant, who was more frightened than I had been; they had to pay him over and above the contracted fee to stop him from blabbing. The other was an opium addict, who could hardly stand straight, and they painted his pale face with lamb black to make him look tough and fearful.

We had to do it, man. We just couldn't stand by and see you riding into hell. We were spying on you all the time and knew the secret goings-on. Now that all that's behind you I hope you will forgive us and understand what we did. If you don't, well that's okay with us, too. We did what we thought was right because you had become a valued friend.

Lionel looked at the window. Through the frosted pane there was the hint of a vague early dawn light. The train whistled and held it long. Lionel sprang to his feet.

Let's get started, he said, and began waking up all the others, pulling them by their feet, digging them in the ribs, and slapping their faces.

Wake up! We're there.

(Dear Lionel! The greatest friend I ever had; Lionel, who dropped out of school after failing the senior exam, gloriously, as he exulted, who didn't care two hoots when he found out that I had been lying about that "London returned" business about my family, that we were actually very poor, but continued to be my friend, went into "creeping" because his father was a planter, got involved with the wife of the plantation's periya dorai, and when he found out that she in turn was sleeping with the sinna dorai, locked himself in his car, put up the shutters, gunned the engine, turned the exhaust inside with a hose pipe stuck through the boot, and slept, never to wake up, on a lonely estate road high up in the tea country, close to where he confessed to me on that night on the cadet train that he was the one who turned those two thugs on me to save me from "Grace Nona's Girl." He was twenty-three.)

The Little Train came whistling to the platform where I was seated on a bench with her hand still on my shoulder, and her question as to why I ran still unanswered, and I felt relieved, because I could never have told her the truth.

I will tell you one day, I said. There's no time now.

I walked her to the train, opened the door, and waited on the platform until she sat down at the window on my side, like they do in films when men and women parted. She wanted me to visit her, where she lived now, towards the east end of the Kelani Valley Line.

She was now living with the man who was with her mother in those days.

The man who ravished her and beat her up until there were welts on her back? How could that be? I wondered.

He looked after me after Mother died.

Yes. I remembered that.

After I ran away from her, she never looked at me, leaped higher in the netball court, ran faster at the sports meet, and wiggled her bum more furiously, challenging everyone to eat their tongues, and then it was time for the term-end vacation. That was the time I walked slowly up the steps of the pavilion towards Lucie Manette who stood on a higher step shining in the sunlight and looking down at me like a reigning queen, and swore I have had nothing to do with *That One* who came from *Over There*.

When the holidays were over, and we came back to school, I had turned seventeen and was deep into my affair with Lucie

Manette, having kissed her behind the black backdrop curtain of the stage while we played a scene from *Hamlet* at the term-end concert.

I heard vaguely that *That One* wasn't coming to school because her mother had died.

She had committed suicide.

The man she was with had got her killed, like the way he got *That One's* father killed.

That One has disappeared.

She is being kept by that man.

Whispered gossip with eyes opening wide and knowing looks, and I didn't dare try to find out or show the least interest, because Lucie Manette would have dropped me like a hot potato.

The Little Train whistled, in that sad long lingering note like a bird calling.

Will you come?

Would that be all right?

Perfectly all right.

I still didn't say yes, and I kept looking at her.

He is quite harmless now; like a vegetable. I look after him like he is a child, she said.

And the Little Train began pulling out of the platform.

It was dark under the rubber trees, and the sad whistle held until the Little Train came out of that gloom into the bright sunlight, and beyond the embankment on the left I saw a strip of paddy, a winding river of emerald green. On either side the undulating land was thickly timbered, and past all that and far away on the patch of blue sky there was a bluer shape like a brush stroke — Sri Pada, the Holy Peak — and it began moving with my angle of vision. I held on to everything that came within sight and floated away, like I wanted to keep my mind tightly closed.

Since waking up in the morning, I had moved from one action to another, like everything had been programmed and I had no choice. I was trapped in the commands of an unseen remote control. I hardly spoke. I had my breakfast silently and dressed and waited until my wife dressed; the taxi I had ordered the previous day came on time. I held my wife by the hand down the stairs of the little flat and into the waiting cab. She was feeling uncomfortable and was restless through the night; this was only the fifth month and there could be no risk of a delivery, not in the fifth month, her mother had declared, looking at me sternly, like I was responsible for her having to come all of the twelve miles she was living away early in the morning. She had disliked me intensely from day one.

The appointment with the doctor was at seven thirty in the morning. He was seeing my wife before going on his ward rounds. He was a morose, unfriendly, non-speaking man, who went about his work like he was irritated. I was seated inside the consultation room while the examination went behind a blue screen; my wife's mother was also behind that screen. It could not have taken more than ten minutes, but I was feeling very tense because I found this whole business of keeping my mind closed very difficult. There was a fear building up within me, that if I let my mind think I would not do what I had been planning to do for well over a month, and I think deep down in me there was a longing to do it. Once more it was that vertigo feeling, where I was suspended between fear and longing.

The doctor came out, and having washed his hands, taking a long time over it, or so I thought, sat at the table and began writing something. I was relieved because now there was something for me to do, and I stood up and placed his fee on the table. Continuing to write with one hand, he opened the drawer with the other, swept the hundred-rupee notes into the drawer, and closed it, never even once looking at the money or at me. He stood up, and still not looking at me, pushed the piece of paper into my hand.

Is there anything wrong, doctor?

He shook his head. Was it "Yes" or "No"? I couldn't tell.

Bring her in a week's time. Till then, give her these tablets.

He pointed vaguely at the piece of paper in my hand, and walked out like he was in a great hurry, and my wife and her mother emerged from behind the screen. The mother looked towards the door from where the doctor had disappeared and then looked at me. There was a scowl on her face as if I had made the doctor disappear.

I looked at my watch; it was not yet seven thirty in the morning. I had already checked for the morning trains on the Kelani Valley Line. There was an east-bound train at eight twenty-five from the nearest railway station, which was only three kilometers from where I was living. I could drop my wife and her mother, and there would still be plenty of time for me to catch the train. I could pretend I was not in a hurry to go wherever I was going. Take it easy. Take your time. But I was nervous. I didn't want to be at home in this state. It would show. The mind would open and start thinking. We stopped at a drug store to get the prescribed tablets. The taxi was going very fast, and I asked the driver to slow down a little.

It is not good for the lady, I told the man. He understood and looked at me apologetically. Good man, I thought to myself. Most taxi drivers wouldn't like to be told how to drive. I settled him with a tip, and he looked pleased. The morning newspaper was lying at the doorstep; I picked it up and began climbing the stairs slowly; my wife and her mother had gone ahead while I was settling the taxi. Walking up the steps as slowly as I could, I tried to read the headline and the other captions on the first page. I saw nothing, and I read nothing. The Little Train whistled far away. It must be crossing the golf links; we heard the train here only when it was crossing that open space, and today it sounded closer than at other times. Once again the mind was trying to break free, like a dog pulling at the leash. I wasn't thirsty, but I opened the fridge and drank water out of a bottle. The water was ice cold, and I had to drink slowly; that was fine because it kept my mind on it for some time. I put the bottle back in the fridge and closed the door. I wanted to go into the bedroom to change my shirt, because it was white, and I wanted to wear something dark that would not collect telltale marks, but the mother was inside the room. My wife came out. She stood near the dining table looking at me, and I kept looking at the paper as if reading it with great interest.

Aren't you getting late?

I heard her say that and looked up.

Yes, but I want to change this shirt, and your mother is there.

Why can't you change your shirt when Mother is there?

Silence. And then I heard her again.

What's wrong with the shirt you are wearing?

This time I thought she sounded like she was curious. Then the mother came out of the room still wearing that scowl, and I went in quickly. My wife came into the room when I was changing my shirt and sat on the bed.

Will you be back for lunch?

No.

Mother is going back. She wants to get back home before dark.

Silence.

Don't get late.

Silence.

I am still not feeling all that good.

Those tablets will take care of that. Doctor said you will be all right.

But don't get late.

Now the Little Train was moving over a bridge, and I was looking out of the window but could not see into the distance through the thick green foliage. There was nothing to hold on to, and I felt my mind break free and begin to think, and the fear came back. I was inside a moving train, and there was nothing I could do but wait until it came to a stop. It will not go back. A bus would be different. You could always ring the bell and get off if you didn't want to go further; get into another bus going the other way and go back. A train is irrevocable. Like time, it only moves forward, no redemption. But wasn't this also a going back? Am I not on some crazy retreat to a point in time past that had receded irreversibly? What brings me on this journey?

The sad whistle rose and fell in a double loop as the Little Train rounded a bend and reached the small station. Two men emerged from the small building made of unshaved granite washed over with white paint and walked lazily to the train. I was the only one to get down, and I had been the only passenger in my compartment. There was an air of desolation here like it was the end of something with nothing beyond. The fear came up the spine and then spread all over me, and I felt a chill like when you have fever. The sad whistle again rising, lingering, falling, and rising again, like some desperate appeal, and with a clash of iron, a lurch, and a spray of pure white steam, the train begins to move, and I keep moving with it along the pavement. I move slowly, and the train begins to pick up speed, pulling away, and it clears the platform before I reach its end. I am alone now at the end of the platform looking towards where the Little Train is disappearing, moving beyond the signal post where the light is green. As the train passes the signal post, I hear footsteps behind and turn round to see a man walking up to a set of levers; one is pulled forward, and the man presses a spring handle and releases it. The lever falls back in line with the other; I turn around to look at the signal post where the light has changed to red. My eyes come back and rest on the country road crossing the rail track at a point beyond the end of the platform. Someone comes along the red gravel road from the left and pauses briefly at the level crossing and then comes almost running towards me along the rail track. As he comes closer, I notice him to be a youth; he is barebodied waist upwards and has a fine physique, and as he gets closer to me he grins, displaying a set of abnormally white teeth, and I know he has come to fetch me.

If you drop me a postcard telling me when you are coming, I could always send someone to the station to meet you. It is a short walk from the station, but on your own you may take the wrong turn.

This is what she told me at the Pettah Station waiting for the train. She told me the address and wanted me to write it down. I didn't. But it was an easy address to remember, and a month later when I decided to come, I still remembered.

Miss V. Ranasighe, she had begun when I interrupted her.

But wasn't your surname Congreve?

Yes, but I changed to my mother's surname.

I thought you loved your father?

That's the very reason I dropped his family name.

I don't understand?

Using his name is unfair. He was such a good man. I have no right to drag his name in the dirt.

She laughed like she had said something funny. I thought I understood what she said.

What does V stand for? I had forgotten.

Don't you remember that at least?

And I suddenly remembered her name was Virginia, and that she had stopped using it because boys had begun calling her Vagina.

The country road, along which I walked with the young man with a fine physique and a set of abnormally white teeth moving slightly ahead of me, crossed a narrow strip of paddy. It was the first month after sowing, and the paddy was blooming in a carpet of tender green. There was the smell of mud and sun-warmed water hanging in the windless air, and it brought back memories. Past this open space where the sky was dull and cloudy the road began moving in shadow; it was cool under the trees and sunless without being gloomy. The fear in me had gone, and I walked looking ahead.

She was by the gate, and we began seeing her from a long way off. It was the young man with me who saw her first.

The Lady is waiting, he said and looked at me flashing his white teeth.

I couldn't see her immediately because she was behind the gate. But as we came closer, she came through the gate and stood, and I could see all of her, wearing a frock falling just below her knees, and a sleeveless blouse that made her look full in front; yet she looked very girlish, very much like *That One* who came from *Over There* in those days. But something of that animation was gone, and there was a calm about her, a settled look. I stopped a few feet before her. The young man walked past her and stood near the gate, and she turned round and looked at him, and he began walking away along the long drive, which moved under coconut trees. At the far end I could see a tiled roof. She walked up and stood very close to me, and I could almost feel the warmth of her body; she was smiling, and she held me by the hand like the way she did when we crossed the road at the Pettah one month ago. She looked happy and surprised as if I had just suddenly materialized.

I thought you wouldn't come.

Why?

Just felt that way.

She took my other hand, too, and I looked around feeling uneasy. That was how we stood in that long ago time before we collapsed on the thin grass on the embankment going down to the strip of paddy beyond which were the rubber trees. Then my heart was pounding and there was in her a desperation to collapse on the ground clinging to me fiercely. But today it was all very different; she held me almost by habit; there was no quickening of reflexes like something had to be gotten over with soon, no urgency, no spasms in her like in those days that sent me wild with urges only half-understood.

I put on my best dress.

She had led me through the gate still holding my hand and then released me to lock the gate. The gate had a padlock. When she finished doing that, she turned round to look at me and smile like she was making sure I was really there.

She took my hand again, and we began to walk along the drive, and it was cool under the coconut trees. There was a mild scent around her, a clean smell of sandalwood or lavender like what is there after a bath. My mind went back again, elsewhere in time, in some other place. Then there was about her some-thing between sweat and some other thing I couldn't quite iden-tify; it would make me a little breathless, and when we collapsed on the thin grass and I always bruised my knees on the hard earth, there came the smell of olive flowers.

Today the clean sandalwood-like scent sedated me. A breeze was coming through the garden and moved around softly under the coconut palms. It was very pleasant.

It is very cool here, I said.

There is a stream flowing right round this garden, she said.

I couldn't see it.

It is down below, flowing under those bamboo groves.

She pointed, and I could see the tops of green bamboo swaying slightly in the slow breeze.

Later, just after high noon and before we had lunch, I sat on a garden bench under the bamboo while she bathed in the stream. The bench was on the slope by a flight of unevenly placed flat stones that led to the stream; at that point there was a large slab of rock surfacing from the water around which the stream flowed. The slab of rock was bleached in patches like when people dash their soaped clothes to wash them. She changed clothes standing on this slab of rock, and I stood on the edge of the slow running stream. The water was clear and you could see the pebbly bottom where fish held against the flow. I kept looking at the fish mostly because I wanted to avoid seeing her change clothes.

Catch this, I heard her say and looked up.

She had already changed into a thin cloth held just above her breasts. The cloth reached up to her knees, and I saw how smooth-skinned and perfectly shaped her calves were; her feet seen through the water were delicate. Dancer's feet, I thought. She had removed the clothes she was wearing and threw them to me in a bundle; I held them, and they had that sandalwood scent with a slight whiff of sweat, and they were still warm with her body heat.

Keep them on the bench, she said, and she watched me hold them in my hands, and there was mischief in her eyes.

That is if you don't want to hold them in your hands.

Then there was that peal of laughter that had made a porter look up at the Fort station. I immediately walked up and deposited them on the bench. That is how I came to be seated there. She was bathing now, dipping under water and coming up; she spread her hands out and cleaved the water as she disappeared under, and when she came up she threw her head back and shook the dark tresses. It was good to watch her because she did not know I was watching. Each time she went down, her cloth billowed and stayed above the water and I knew she was naked underneath. Going by the calves and the delicate dancer's feet and the smooth skin below the knees, she should be the same up there. I had forgotten, or was it that I had never known?

We had sat in the veranda that encircled the house on three sides talking for a long time. It was an old manor house, and the broad veranda opened out to the garden of large shade trees taking the glare out of the sun. It was cool and pleasant talking with her in that open space and looking at all the green around. It was my idea to sit there. As I stepped into the house, I saw the dark interior, the furniture shrouded in white to keep off the dust, the walls on either side going deep towards the back with the doors to the rooms closed, and I knew that in one of those closed rooms *That Man* would be there. She had told me at the Fort station, waiting for the train, that he had become a vegetable. I didn't want to ask her for details, because the very thought of her living alone with that "vegetable" made me feel sick. When I met her at the gate and saw her waiting for me, and she looked so attractive and vulnerable, I immediately thought of the "vegetable" that she was "looking after." Horrible thoughts flashed across my mind, and I felt sick once more. But then that sandalwood scent sedated me until I walked into that veranda and through the large multipaned door, saw that cavernous interior receding far into the back. And I knew that behind one of those closed doors the "vegetable" would be lying, rotting slowly. Maybe it was watching us through some crack or a chink in the wall of his room. I imagined that I got the odor of death coming from within that house and decided firmly then and there that I was going to stay in the veranda, looking at all that herbaceous splendor surrounding this house while somewhere within a man was slowly rotting. Perhaps it was her freshness that made the situation so very depressing.

I recovered slowly, because she sat with her chair drawn close to me, tapped on my shoulder or pressed my hand to make a point, and regularly there came that laugh, pealing like a bell. Two glasses of chilled fresh orange juice—plucked from the garden, she said—poured from a crystal decanter, its top covered with a cloth of delicate white lace with tassels with colored beads hanging on the ends, made me feel good.

We spoke of many things, and there were certain things we instinctively avoided, until she said her mother had died.

That was when I stopped school, she said.

Was it true she committed suicide?

My mother? No. She would never commit suicide. She liked the good things of life. Would have given anything to have them.

I noticed a tinge of bitterness in her voice, and it was unusual in someone who looked back on everything with a laugh.

How did she die?

I shouldn't have asked that question, I thought immediately after, and she looked away from me. She kept closing and opening her fist very slowly like she was making a mudra and looked pensive. I had not seen her like that since I met her in the Pettah after twelve years. Perhaps I had not seen her like that even in those days when she came from *Over There*.

She didn't commit suicide.

How then? I wanted to ask, but kept silent, and she immediately switched key. Her voice had regained that friendly and playful tone when she asked me, What happened with Subhadra?

Once more I took time to remember. Subhadra was "Lucie Manette," the proud one who played the piano and spoke in English like it was her mother tongue.

It didn't last too long.

Why?

She was too much for me.

And I told her the story of my short-lived affair with Subhadra, alias "Lucie Manette," which began on the steps of the pavilion when she stood there in a bright sunbeam, dazzling like a reigning queen looking down on me, and ended on a rainy day at a railway crossing when I was on a bicycle wet like a crow and she was in the front seat of a car with a dashing young man at the wheel, and she accidentally looked my way, saw me, and immediately began looking far away until the rail gates opened and the traffic began to move.

I didn't want to tell her that I cried secretly for weeks, wrote two long letters pouring out my grief that were returned through a friend, and a few months later after the senior examination she left school and went back to Kandy because her father had managed to get transferred there, and that I continued to pine for her for another year, during which time I had began to lose interest in school. I also didn't want to tell her that I had felt a certain cooling off on the part of Subhadra before that moment at the railway crossing, because she was always late for our trysts, where nothing much happened and nothing much was said, and she was always in a hurry to go. Perhaps it was that I did not smell of Old Spice, wore no Arrow shirts with stiff collars, had no car at home, and she had slowly realized I was of an inferior brand.

There ensued a silence as if we were thinking of what else to talk about. It was close to high noon, but still cool in the veranda with all that green outside, and I began to notice how well-swept the garden was; there wasn't a leaf on the nicely trimmed grass that was all around, with only the gravel path running up to the house. In the portico was a large car, a black Mercedes-Benz with all four tires deflated, and it looked like it had not been on the road for years. I heard the sound of activity in the back of the house, pails being kept on the ground and the handles being dropped with a clang, female voices talking all at once. The tappers have finished their work for the morning, she said. There is forty acres of rubber here, she continued, several rubber rolling machines and a large smoke room. There are nearly a hundred tappers, mostly women, who have to be paid at the end of the day. When I wanted to know who managed all this, she smiled sweetly and pointed to herself. I wanted to ask something else when there came from within the house something like the dying groan of a large animal. It began with a rattle, rose up, and died down like an engine refusing to get started. Then it started all over again, and she stood up.

It's him, she said and walked quickly into the dark inside the house. I heard the creak of a door, and then there was silence. For me there was a threat in that sound, and also something evil, and I wanted to run; run all the way along the pathway through the coconut palms and out over that locked gate; run somewhere for the second time to escape a pursuing terror. But just then that young man with a fine physique and white teeth appeared from a side of the house; his magnificent torso was bathed in sweat like he had been doing some hard labor. He flashed his teeth at me and stood there as if he wanted to talk. I noticed he was very fair with a reddish tint and had the face of a child. He just stood there looking at me blankly; he was not even curious, but was just standing there because he knew nothing else to do, and he was making me nervous. I was relieved when she reappeared, and the young man began moving away aimlessly like a stray dog.

Before sitting down, she placed a hand on my shoulder, and

I noticed it was washed and there were wet patches up to her elbows. She kept wiping her other hand on her skirt, and I got the smell of carbolic soap.

I saw you getting alarmed, she said. That is how he calls me. He cannot talk.

What does he call you?

He used to call me Cuckoo, but now it is only a sound when he calls. Only I understand it. I know what he is calling me for each time, there are variations, now he wanted the bed pan.

She sat down and swept her hair back.

I remembered the name Cuckoo. I used to call her by that name in those days, but only when the two of us were alone; I never referred to her by that pet name with others if I referred to her at all, and all my letters were addressed to "My Cuckoo." She had told me to call her by that name, because that was what her father had called her, and each time I called her Cuckoo, she felt it was her father calling her from somewhere.

The voice from within the house called for Cuckoo twice. To me it sounded like "GlrrrooooogoOOOooooo." The second time he called she wanted me to come with her. When I hesitated, she said it is all right because he cannot see anything, and I followed her through the hall sunk in gloom with the furniture shrouded in white, and I felt that rancid smell of death. The door creaked as she opened it, and there came from within the overpowering smell of herbal oil and urine and feces. But nothing had prepared me for what I saw. On the iron bed lying on a canvas, the color of stale blood, was something like a huge spider with oily limbs sticking up every which way and stark naked. I couldn't see the head immediately; it was somewhere in the tangle of spidery limbs. It was a shriveled nut, little more than a skull. The eyes were wide open, unblinking and glazed, and saw nothing. She picked up a feeding bottle and added what appeared to be orange juice and kept the teat on his lips;

the mouth was only a line, and she searched for the lips with her fingers, wetting the almost invisible lip line with orange juice, and she slowly opened his lips by inserting the rubber teat. The sunken cheeks on the skull moved slightly and began to suck. The eyes dilated. There was another bed in the room kept against the wall with clean white linen and pillows. Thrown carelessly on the bed was a cloth with a vague floral pattern. Quite close to the bed was a half-closed door through which I could see the bathroom. The sucking stopped, and as the teat was pulled out, the mouth began to dribble. She wiped the lips with a discolored serviette lying on the table near the bed and walked into the bathroom.

I walked out.

The odors followed me through the gloomy hall into the veranda. The light outside the garden had brightened, and there were bright patches of sun under the trees. The wind had dropped, and everything was still and quiet, and the air was getting warmer. I had stopped thinking and was looking around for things to hang on to; the need to keep the mind closed was there again, but the evil odors from the room where there was a broken spider with oily limbs, stiff and pointed like dead twigs, was still clinging to me, making me feel uneasy.

She came out stepping lightly and gracefully, and once more there came with her the sanitized scent of carbolic soap. I was seated on a chair on the edge of the veranda looking into the gloomy hall, and she stood by me facing the garden. We waited in silence for some time. I wondered whether her taking me into the room was some form of revenge. It was something like the way she leapt higher and ran faster after I had abandoned her. But now it was more subtle, more understated. Standing by my side and looking silently into the sunlit garden, I felt she was waiting for me to say something.

Do you sleep in that room?

She rested a hand gently on my shoulder, but kept looking into the garden.

I have to.

Can't you hire someone to do it?

I can't do that.

Why?

I feel good when I do it, like I'm purifying myself.

I thought of something to say, and she sat on the floor of the veranda with her feet on the ledge by the rainwater drain. Now her head was on a level with the armrest of my chair. She was still looking away into the garden.

Can you stand all that mess inside the room?

One gets used to things.

Once more I thought she was trying to hurt me, make me feel bad for letting this happen to her; the revulsion I felt in that evil-smelling room was being replaced by something else. I was feeling uneasy like I do when I've done something foul. The silence with her sitting so close to me was slowly becoming unbearable. The air had become warm and heavy, and it was not pleasant in the veranda any more.

"Glrrroooogooooooooooo!"

She didn't move at first; she stood still, like it was no concern of hers, looking at the garden slowly warming in the noonday heat. The voice called again, and she stood up slowly and began walking into the gloom inside the hall, keeping her face averted all the time. The way she walked with her head bent, I felt she was crying and didn't want me to see. Halfway into the gloom, I saw her wipe her face with the back of her hand. The door creaked, and then it clicked shut. Near where she had been seated by the side of my chair with her legs outstretched towards the rainwater drain, the smell of carbolic soap lingered.

She came back quickly this time, and her eyes were smiling again.

Are you hungry?

No, I said.

It was then that she suggested a bath in the stream. For me that would have been the ultimate risk. I would have carried in me the scent of some soap — sandalwood most probably — and that would be disastrous. When I grinned and hesitated, she looked amused.

Scared your lady would know?

Yes, I said. I had to be honest at least now.

He may call for you again, I said as we were walking through a large green bamboo grove towards the stream.

He won't, she said. Not for another few hours.

How do you know?

I gave him a sleeping pill.

The dipping and rising in the stream had stopped; when she did that occasionally after soaping herself, the cloth did not billow anymore; it clung to her, making her look very naked. Her body was in full bloom, and there was an opulence of line along the thighs, and I tried to remember her in those days when we lay in the thin grass, and the smell of olive flowers came back, a whiff from the past. We had, in those moments of the past, always been in a horizontal position, with her white frock pulled up, and whenever we stood up, she always pulled the hemline down to cover the legs, and I was always in a hurry to end the proceedings before someone appeared on the edge of the playground. There were a few times when she was wearing a separate top with a skirt divided between the legs to play netball, and on a few such occasions when we were together she opened the top in front and offered her breasts for me to fondle, and once in a frenzy I had pulled the top over her head, and that was when I saw the welts on her back caused by the man who was now rotting in a stinking mess and looking like a huge broken spider with oily limbs upstruck like dried twigs and being fed by her with a feeding bottle. Could all these things belong together? They did, and that was what was disturbing me, making me feel sick.

She came out of the stream, stepping lightly on the strip of pebbles along the water's edge, and she stood on the grass under the green bamboo. The sun had turned slightly beyond noon, the slanting light was behind her. That is another image I carry of her—backlit softly with water dripping along the long strands of hair falling all over her shoulders, and breasts still firm and upturned under the wet cloth, a wafer-thin sheath clinging to every curve and hollow of a body in full bloom. She stood there, still and motionless for a moment, like an erotic sculpture. The foul smells that had followed me like an evil spirit from that room where a man lay rotting in his own shit and discharges vanished, and I felt clean again.

Lunch was laid out on a back veranda that opened out into a central courtyard, swept clean once again, with an old bird bath in the center. Across the courtyard on the opposite wing was the cooking area with smoke from slow wood fires in the kitchen bringing warm smells of rich country food. There were two women busy in the kitchen, and one kept bringing things to the table until we began eating. It was a long table with antique chairs with curved headrests making us very comfortable. A cat had come from somewhere, a big roguelike tabby who kept rubbing against her legs, meowing gutturally. We ate slowly and spoke little, like two people perfectly at ease with each other. She kept serving me, like she was happy doing it.

Once we finished, one of the women from the kitchen began clearing the table. The other woman brought a large bowl filled with mangoes. Cuckoo went inside the house and came back with a knife. The woman clearing the table brought two fresh plates. The mangoes looked good. They were yellow with red patches. Cuckoo put a plate in front of me and began peeling a mango with the knife. She was standing very close to me, and after the bath she smelled of sandalwood again like earlier in the morning before she went inside that room and came back with a carbolic smell. She was slicing the mango after peeling and dropping the slices on my plate. Each time she did that she pressed against my shoulder. I knew it was not calculated. She had become free with me, as if our relationship had continued without a break. And anything she did looked natural and totally without guile.

This is the best mango I have ever tasted, I said.

This is a very special hybrid. Only we have it around here.

She started peeling another one.

I will give you some to take home to your lady.

Whenever she referred to my wife, it was "Your Lady." She was not mocking either. I suppose she wanted to be polite or perhaps formal. In Sinhala the polite word for wife sounds too false and affected, and the colloquial term, which is just "Your Woman," sounds too disrespectful.

It was more than cool under the rubber trees, and the breeze moving swiftly around carried with it the smell of rain. We were walking on the edge of the rubber land along a footpath, which ran parallel to the stream. The sound of flowing water came from below where the stream was. We could not see it because of the water plants with large leaves lining the stream. She was walking me to the railway station along a footpath through the rubber land. There were no rubber trees beyond a certain point, and we began walking through woodland. There was no undergrowth here, and the ground was wet and spongy with dead leaves from the large trees. Through the trees I could now see the telegraph poles and the wires along them on the rail track.

Along the rail track there were no trees, and the telegraph poles stood against a bleak gray sky. She had held on to my hand all along, and in her other hand she carried a bag full of mangoes for "Your Lady." She did not let me carry it. Now the track we were following sloped down to a lower level before it turned to cross the stream and go up to the rail track. In a sudden throwback to adolescence, we held hands and ran down the slope, breaking to a halt just before we took the turn to go up towards the rail track. We could not see the rail track anymore, and only the tops of the telegraph poles stood against the gray sky. We kept looking at each other, laughing like two kids having fun. There was something artificial about that run, something put on like we were playing for time holding back what had been coming inevitably from morning when we looked at each other near the gate. The laughter ended abruptly, and then came the final pause, the quivering moment of suspense. We tore at each other, collapsing on the wet spongy ground, thrashing wildly like two mating cobras, exploring each other all over with hands and mouths until she began restraining and guiding me to a gentle rhythm, delaying and prolonging, and then a slow build up again to reach the blinding consummation of a longing held back so cruelly all this time.

The train whistled rising in a crescendo to a heart-rending cry almost musical in its sadness, and it was like waking from a long, healing slumber as I regained my senses, and the Little Train thundered just above us, unseen but sounding like a thousand iron wheels on iron.

Isn't that the train?

What I meant was whether it wasn't the train I was supposed to take back home.

Yes, she said, and when I wanted to get up she held me back firmly upon her.

There is another one coming in twenty minutes' time.

Her hands and legs wrapped around me, and I went limp again.

The station is just here.

The train that went by was the three fifty-five from this station, and the next one, if it came on time, would be at four fifteen and would take me back to my station in approximately one hour's time. The Little Train was also a slow train; I would be happy to be home before dark.

Would you come again?

Yes, I said, but I knew I would not.

Come whenever you feel it is safe — safe for you — it is always safe for me here. Even if it is not, I don't care.

I care, I said to myself.

Come before it is too late, she said again. You will have children in due time, then it would be difficult for you to come, and it would be wrong of me to ask you. Give me a few times with you before that.

I will, I said, but knew I never could.

As I walked along the rail track towards the station all alone now, I looked back to where I left her. That place was now hidden among the giant leaves of the water plants along the stream, but I knew she would still be there. Perhaps she was crying. She always cried alone, without being seen, even in those days. From where she was, crying perhaps, beyond those water plants, she couldn't see me either.

I had the bag of mangoes in my hand. I stopped and swung it around my head several times and released it to go as far as it would. There was a marsh on the other side of the rail track where it fell with the dull thud of something heavy dropping on soft mud.

To take those mangoes home would be unfair to both women, I thought.

1985. London.

It was a cold afternoon in November. A feel of winter had come long before its scheduled arrival, and London was expecting snow. There was in me a sense of fulfillment as I walked slowly down Shaftesbury Avenue. The glint was gone from the autumn's light, and the day was closing fast, and in the crowds flowing every which way there was a hurry like in homing birds. I walked slowly. I had come all the way from Bush House, straight up Kingsway to High Holborn, and then falling into this path was moving towards Charing Cross Road. Now that was my favorite way in this city, a path I had been slowly tracing over three visits in just two years. Walking southwards with the top of Nelson's Column always visible like a guiding star, I could stop at the second-hand book shops all the way to Leicester Square and then down into Trafalgar, or proceed straight on Shaftesbury Avenue past London Trocadero to Piccadilly and wait and watch and walk about with Eros constantly as a center, until I could walk down Haymarket, once again to where the pigeons were.

I was always a pilgrim, and I was reclaiming, perhaps, some imaginary space that had grown and taken shape in my mind, long before I set eyes on it. It had grown out of the peculiar circumstances of my adolescence in which I had to invent myths, nurse them carefully just to keep going, so as not to be marked and thrown out of the herd. It was the survival instinct of the silkworm weaving its cocoon. Wasn't I "born here" in that story about myself I had maintained so blasphemously once-upon-a-long-ago-time? Most of those I knew and grew up with back home had come here long before I did, and they came for very practical purposes: to study, to make money, to see the place because their parents could afford to do so, or just to wash dishes, pump gas, deliver newspapers in the winter and return home with plenty of money and an accent and mannerisms, such as the lifting of the shoulders to make a point. In me there had always been a fear of going. I had to wait until I was winged to break open the cocoon; or was it that it had become a permanent habit of self-deception? Perhaps there was the fear of losing the dream; of the phantom rainbow evaporating in the real. Walking London, I was in search of myself, trying to make it all come true.

On that late autumn afternoon with the day beginning to die, and the edge gone from the light, and the crowds homing, and in no hurry to get anywhere, I had this feeling that I was out of my cocoon; that I was free of something at last, and I felt the wings lifting me up. That was the sense of fulfillment with which I walked. I did not know I was on Charing Cross Road until I was halfway down towards Leicester Square. I was on it like an animal moving along its path by instinct. I may have walked it first because of the bookstalls, but it was on this road that I had first felt easy in this city. Walking along here I began to know where I was, and in my mind's eye could see the whole of London from Regent's Park, to across the Thames all the way to its south bank. There, too, I walked along the embankment, crossing the Waterloo Bridge, pausing to look at the river in homage to Eliot — *Sweet Thames, run softly . . . etc. etc.* — until I reached the National Film Theatre under the bridge to spend, sometimes, the whole day watching movies, and when the night was too far gone to walk, I would catch the tube on the Northern Line to connect to the purple line at Leicester Square to reach my home at Sudbury Hill. Evenings I was mostly subterranean, moving silently under like a burrowing animal, but the city above would still be in me like it was in the day.

Fonseka!

I kept walking before I heard it almost on the rebound like in an echo.

I stopped. I could see the Leicester Square tube station, spilling people and drawing them in from all three sides. I turned around, and I could still see Eros pissing naughtily.

But from where did that call come? It was from the bowels of a past I was thirty years away from as I was walking on a London street with the night coming fast on a late autumn afternoon and the day going cold with the threat of an early winter and the feel of coming snow.

I stood still on the passenger walk, like I had been fixed there by some evil mantram; a moment in the middle of a lap dissolved, like in a movie when something was fading out and something else coming in and both were visible at the same time.

Fonseka!

It called again, and on the other side across the road a hand went up slowly. It was of a man, and I saw the head first, wearing a Stetson tilted slightly to a side, then the elegant mohair overcoat staying easy on the shoulders, open in the front, revealing a vertical strip of pin-striped tweed. The other hand went up, too, in a gesture like he wanted me to stay where I was, as he kept walking towards the pedestrian crossing further up on the road, and I didn't stay where I had stopped but kept walking parallel on my side trying all the time to think who this could be. The easy swaggering stride was vaguely familiar, and I was sure he was from that uneasy twilight of my adolescence when I went to school, because that was the time I was known by my paternal surname, and all my friends knew me as Fonseka before I dropped out of school and wanted to become a writer—and I was writing in the vernacular at the time—my guru, the revered Professor Sarachcandra, wanted me to drop my Portuguese family name because he himself was a De Silva, and he had changed it, and I became what I became to be, a Sinhala writer. The man in a Stetson who hailed me in my now long-forgotten Portuguese name, and who was walking on the other side of the road, stopped at the pedestrian crossing. We were waiting for the green to cross. Beneath the hat he was brown, I noticed, and he looked like an Indian millionaire. The green came, and I wanted to cross, but the two hands went up again wanting me to wait, and he came across the road; a big man with an easy walk; like a retired boxer, I thought.

Good to see you, man. I wasn't so sure. But now I know it is you.

He shook me mightily, gripping me by the shoulders until my teeth almost rattled.

Soli.

Solomon Reginald de Zoysa, alias Soli.

A bodybuilder who would split the sleeves of his shirt by stiffening his biceps, get a hard-on at will in his trousers and, placing a book on it, would keep tossing it visibly under the desk while calmly looking at the teacher explaining logarithms and pretending fierce concentration. Distinguished member of the "dirty gang" I was hanging out with a raving homosexual, once caught fondling a middle-school boy and got away by explaining quite convincingly that he was giving the boy a rub because the little fellow had a cramp. And now, nearly thirty years later, walking calmly across Charing Cross Road, wearing a mohair overcoat and a Stetson on the head tilted rakishly, looking like an Indian millionaire, to shake me by the shoulders, hugely pleased. It was Soli all right, and all of him all over again.

Soli's voice boomed with laughter and then roared when I told him I was no longer Fonseka, and the late afternoon tipplers at the pub looked at us and frowned.

For me it helped to continue as Zoysa here, he said. I convinced these buggers my ancestor came from Corsica, and he roared again, and again the drinkers looked up displeased.

I couldn't immediately remember where Corsica was, and he explained.

Some fucking little island somewhere, we were told—can't you remember?—by that bugger (now who was it who taught us European history, ah yes, Ariyaratne, who grinned like a monkey and we called him Wandura)—that Napoleon Bonaparte came from.

It is near Italy, I said having remembered where it was, but he wasn't interested. He was on his third big mug of draught beer, and I was on my second scotch. He called for more drinks.

Soli was settled down in Birmingham, and he was a property developer and came to London only once a fortnight. On business, he said. But I felt he had other biological interests.

Halfway through his fourth beer, when I was still on my second scotch, he suddenly remembered something and brought his mug down hard on the table.

Do you remember Jane?

Who?

That girl you buggered who came from across the paddy field? The one everyone did something with?

Yes.

You remember, don't you?

Yes.

I think we also called her Vagina, because her real name was Virginia, or some such thing. Remember?

Yes, I said, and kept my eyes firmly on the drink.

Then I will tell you a story, and he told me, gulping more beer, not getting drunk but roaring like a randy bull, and the men around the other tables getting to look more and more angry, and it was becoming difficult for me to keep staring at my glass because it was empty, and having to fill it up more than I would like to, and my head beginning to go heavy not so much from the drink.

He took time telling his story, like he was rolling something good in his tongue, enjoying every moment of it, and wanting to prolong the pleasure. When he finished, and we walked out into the street, night had come. He was going towards Covent Garden, he said, because his car was parked there, and he was going to drive through the night back to Birmingham. He wanted me to walk with him up to his car, but I said I needed to get back fairly early in the night to where I was staying, which was not true, and he gave me his card. He was coming back here the following week and wanted me to buzz him to fix up a meeting. We could spend more hours going over old times. I agreed, but I knew I would be gone by then, and felt happy about that. I watched him as he walked away in the unreal glow of the streetlights. I walked inside the Leicester Square tube station but came out again from another exit and began walking down St. Martin's Lane. At the church down there an orchestra was playing. I recognized it as something from Liszt, and it wafted sweetly through the cold. Now I was ready to recover the story my friend from the past had told me, to redeem it from the bawdiness at the pub, and the beer-soaked guffaws through which it came, and this seemed the right place to do it because of the music coming from the churchyard.

Soli's story went something like this:

Sometime in the late sixties, or perhaps it was the early seventies—he wasn't sure—he had come back home for a brief holiday; his brother-in-law had proposed he buy a forty-acre stretch of rubber land going cheap. He wasn't sure he was going to invest in real estate back home, but when he saw the place he fell for it immediately; it was on the Kelani Valley railroad, just where the hills began and with a stream flowing all around and an old manor house right in the middle. A man had lived there with his young mistress, and when he died after a long illness, the man's two sons from his legal wife had come and thrown the mistress out of the house and closed up the place. The two sons had threatened to burn her alive if she ever protested or went to courts. They were powerful men and quite ruthless, and the woman had vanished, Soli's brother-in-law suspected she could have been murdered. The deal was closed within two days.

It was a huge bargain, man.

Soli's voice boomed again triumphantly.

And then, Soli had continued the story, two days later he was in his hotel in Colombo when the reception called to say there was a visitor for him. He came down to see a woman, who, according to him, looked like a cheap streetwalker waiting for him. She looked in terrible shape, like someone who had walked for days without food; an attempt to cover such ravages with lipstick made her look more dilapidated.

She tried to introduce herself, said Soli, and I wasn't getting through when she said "Jane" and smiled. Man, it was that one in school with us who came from across the paddy fields who everyone did something with. Well, to be frank, I wasn't surprised. The way she was going on, we all knew she would end up on the streets. She was the one who had been kept by that man in the house I had bought with the forty acres of rubber and a stream running round it.

She was in hiding, she said; those two men were searching for her, and she wanted to get out of the country, and she wanted a little money for the ticket.

So did you give it to her? That was the only time I spoke during the long narration.

You think I am nuts? Soli was not booming this time but looking serious.

Why?

Such women mean trouble.

He drained the mug and put it down and called for the check. Then he spoke again.

I asked her to come the next morning.

He paused to get his Gold Card, and I was waiting.

She may have come. But I was already on my early morning flight back to the U.K.

Liszt's symphonic poem played by a small amateur orchestra continued behind me as I turned away from the church yard of Saint Martin's in the Fields. The lights on the Strand on my left arced gracefully along Eliot's river, and the pigeons were cooing in their holes around Nelson's Column; traffic lights swirled in a carnival round Trafalgar.

I thought of home; a four-year-old daughter was waiting for a special Christmas present, and my wife was with child again; she was expecting a son; a son for me after two failed marriages and four daughters would be great, but if it's a girl again, that would be fine, too. At last there was a happy home waiting for me to return to, and today, walking down Charing Cross, I had carried with me a sense of fulfillment, a feeling of wings lifting me up at last. But now I was grounded again. Like the homing crowds quickening to get back to roost before dark, I wanted desperately to be home.

But that was elsewhere.

And here, now, something was happening.

People had suddenly stopped in their movements and were all looking up. From the vaulting dark up above, snow had begun to fall; it fell in tiny flakes, vaguely seen against the dark above the lights, and then sparkling as it fell against the street lamps. The wisps of pure white came swaying and hovering with a gentle hiss and a whispering sibilance, and from the people stilled in wonder down below there arose an equally soft heaving sigh of pleasure.

It was my first snow in London. But beyond the falling white there lurked splashes of red tropical sunlight on pools of water here and there on a paddy field bare after the harvest, and after that the red of a dying day bathed the tops of rubber trees.

That was elsewhere again.

She was crossing the strip of bare paddy field red in patches in the dying day, and she was a speck of white dissolving in the dark under the rubber trees and the voices from the playground above — or was it the sound of pigeons?

The day had died at last, and the dark moved over everything, covering the strip of paddy, and the antennae sticking up like dried twigs where once there were rubber trees had disappeared, but in my mind's eye the girl in the white uniform was still crossing the strip, bathed in gold as I turned to leave. The playground was in the dark, but at the other edge there were lights in the hostel; the olive tree was gone, and there was a large patch of sky there, and daylight lingered on it, gray and cadaverous. I should have walked up to the hostel and thanked the warden who gave me permission to wander around; but I found myself turning away in the middle of the playground, where the cricket pitch was, and walking towards the pavilion. Behind the pavilion roof on the high ground where the buildings were, the garden lights had come. It was dark, though, on the steps leading up to the pavilion, but I saw the beam of sunlight where Subhadra stood like a reigning queen, waiting for me to come up to her — elsewhere in time.

Now I was crossing the netball court, where once again, elsewhere in time, she was leaping like a colt, and I came down the steps between the office block and the main hall out into where the temple trees stood, and they were heavy with white blossoms as they always were. It was good to feel the delicate fragrance of those flowers hanging in the air. Two globes were burning at the shrine room. It would have been good to remove my shoes and walk across the sand and then up the steps to gaze briefly at the beautiful statue of the Samadhi Buddha within the shrine room. It was purely for aesthetic pleasure. Faith had gone away from me long ago. Yet I felt unclean to go up there. I did not belong to the scent of these pure white flowers cleansing the air and the Samadhi statue casting its serene look around. I had betrayed, and I had despoiled, and there was in me a deep guilt like in someone who has taken life. Wasn't I of the herd that sacrificed a calf to the predator to survive and get on?

I looked towards the old tuck shop; I could see my car there because it was white. The tuck shop, where Lionel and Suren had once waited for me, was only a shadow behind the car.

Could anything be redeemed?

No.

Everything was elsewhere.

Hark, the Moaning Pond

–

A Grandmother's Tale

My mother's ancestral roots on her maternal side were in the central hills of the island where there was a small independent mountain kingdom, which the British annexed by a treaty in 1815. The British called this kingdom Kandy, an abbreviation of a local name that meant The Five Lands up in the Hills. My mother was born in Colombo, but her mother—my grandmother—came from up there. A young Buddhist monk had disrobed himself to elope with my grandmother. She had been a girl of sixteen. She and the Buddhist monk, dressed as a layman with his shaven head covered in a turban, which, according to the story coming down through family lore, he never even once removed throughout the entire journey of two weeks, had joined a group of pilgrims going to the Holy Peak—Sri Pada. They climbed it from the eastern side in the central hills of the island and came down on the western slope to the Kelani Valley, a vast plain of paddy fields snaking around the mountain ridges all the way to the sea. The Buddhist monk was from a village somewhere on the edge of those rice paddies, closer to the city of Colombo. He became my grandfather. He died before my mother was born. By the time he died my grandmother already had two children from him, a boy and a girl. My mother was the third and not yet born. My grandmother never went back to her village in the mountains. But after the death of her husband, she moved with her two kids and the one yet to be born to Colombo. Why she left her husband's village is not clearly established. There are many stories. It was so long ago—in the second decade of the twentieth century—and no one is sure now.

In Colombo, my grandmother lived in a row of tenements in a suburb where my mother was born. In the tenements lived the first generation of people who had moved from all over the country to the city in search of work. They were still not completely city folk. These were the people who went back to their villages during the harvest moon of the Sinhala New Year in April. The men worked in the Port of Colombo and in the factories and warehouses coming up along the waterfront and near the Great Ferry, where a great bridge named after Queen Victoria crossed the big river Kelani, flowing through the valley of green rice paddies where my grandfather's village was, and to which he came back from a temple in the hills with a sixteen-year-old Kandyan girl, and also around the shores of the Beira—a girdle of water that severed the Fort of Colombo from the rest of the city.

How my grandmother sustained her brood in the early years in the city is the subject of many stories. One has it that she brought with her a fistful of gems, which she always kept hidden in her waist, and sold one gem each month, and the stock lasted for two years. Her husband, my grandfather—the ex-Buddhist-monk—had gone into gem mining and was doing pretty well when he died. About his death, too, there are many versions. According to one, he was killed. Why? No one knows for sure. What happened to all the other gems he would have had in the house—grandmother brought only a fistful—and his other property which, if he was a gem miner, would have been extensive, too, has gone into the realm of myth and legend.

Most of what I know about my mother's family is what I have heard and may not be entirely true. I did not hear them in any sequence either, and certain things were never discussed openly between elders in my family. I picked them up by eavesdropping, pretending to be fast asleep or looking the other way when the elders gossiped. I may have arranged what I heard in some kind of order to give them the meaning I wanted. That is why I say that what I am going to say may not be entirely true. I like to tell stories, to connect the dots and create a picture. The dots may also connect in some other way and create a totally different picture.

Some things, however, are true. It is true that my grandmother already had a son and a daughter before my mother was born. The son went to work in a textile mill—when he was sixteen and the stock of his mother's gems had run out—where he rose up to be the chief machine binder and a trade union leader. The Wellawatta Spinning and Weaving Mills, first owned by the Nizam of Hyderabad of India and later by a company of Parsees from Bombay, survived into the seventies, its tall chimney spewing smoke at all times of the day and seen from any part of the city, and its siren heard within fifteen miles. My mother, who would have grown up with that siren in her ears, would make me listen to it when we were living twelve miles away. She measured her day by that distant call. For me it was a sound vague and distant when heard at home. But whenever Father took me to his ancestral home, from where across a broad expanse of coconut land at the end of which was a public park I could see the mill and its tall chimney smoking throughout the day, the sound of that siren was like a great booming foghorn, which frightened me.

My uncle, the one who went to work at the Spinning and Weaving Mills when grandmother ran out of her gems, lived until I was into my early twenties. He loved my mother very much and called her "Little One." I think he also loved me, for he once made me a wooden car, which I could pedal. The pedal of that car was improvised out of a bicycle. When he came over, my mother would not sit down in front of him. I think he was her surrogate father. I remember him always in immaculate white with a red shawl loosely thrown round his neck. But he came very rarely, because my mother's people were not very welcome in our home. When they came, they entered from the back, and if my father was at home, they spoke in whispers and left quickly.

My aunt—my grandmother's other daughter who was already there when my mother was born—is still living. She is very old and has since become a child. I like to think of her as a child because that's how I last saw her, when she kept smiling and crying in turn like infants do in their sleep. Looking at her child's face, very fair and much wrinkled yet beautiful, I remembered something my mother used to say. "My sister was very beautiful in her youth, the most beautiful young woman I have ever seen." Looking at my aunt I tried to picture in my mind the beautiful young woman my mother had spoken about. Then I remembered my grandmother. I think my aunt resembled her mother—my grandmother—as I remembered.

Grandmother's face is one of my earliest memories. She died when I was five, in 1944, a year before the war ended. There is a story around her death too.

She had returned from a pilgrimage to the Holy Peak—the same place she went purporting to be a pilgrim when she eloped with the Buddhist monk who covered his shaven head for two weeks to hide himself—and on the day after her return came to see me. Whenever this story is told it is stressed that she came to see me. Once a week she would come, Mother used to say, mainly to see me. She lived with her son in the north-end of the city, which was fifteen miles from where we lived. To see me she had to come by two trains. The first one brought her to the Central Station in Colombo. From there she would board the southeast-bound narrow gauge train, which moved along the Kelani Valley all the way up to a terminal on the western slopes of the country—the same slopes along which my grandfather descended with his sixteen-year-old girl from the hills—

near the Holy Peak. From Central Station grandmother traveled twelve miles on this train to a station half a mile from our house. From there she would walk to our place, and sometimes on hot days, she would hire Thomas's buggy cart, which was always there by the railroad for passengers.

I can remember the day she came to see me on her return from the pilgrimage to the Holy Peak. I can't remember her arriving, but I can remember her seated by the bay window on the upper level of our house where there was an easy chair. I was seated on her lap, and looking out of the window I could see over and beyond the treetops in our back compound to the sun on the rice paddies. I was trying to tell Grandmother that I could, on some days, see the Holy Peak in the sky, beyond the rice paddies from here. It was pleasant on Grandmother's lap. Her sari, white with purple flowers—or was it blue?—and worn in the style of hill-country women, was crisp and clean of freshly laundered starch, and there was about her the smell of perfumed oil and betel with areca nut and cardamom. I remember the warmth of her face against mine.

The next thing I see in my memory is Grandmother near the front gate—the blue wooden gate with the grill of the rising sun and always closed except when Father's people came in their big cars—and Carolis, the servant boy, trying to open it. I was in the veranda with Mother looking across the porch and through the palm tree. I had never seen Grandmother come or go through that gate. Her people—my mother's people—always came from the gate of zinc sheets at the back. But this day it was different. Perhaps that's why I remember it. The story is that Grandmother went away offended by something I had said. I had walked up to her with a discarded leather bag and offered it to her saying, "Good for Grandma to carry beef in." I can't remember doing that, but I must have. Grandmother had alleged my mother put me up to do that. I don't remember

Mother doing that either. Now there's a point to all this. Grand-mother would observe Sil regularly on the day of the full moon. But she had a partiality to beef. A pious temple-going woman eating beef! It was an in-joke in her family. If I did what I was supposed to have done, it was natural Grandmother was offended, especially when she had just returned from a pilgrimage to the Holy Peak. I can't remember any of this now, but having heard it repeatedly over the years, it is taken for granted that I said what I was supposed to have said, and Grandmother went away offended. But I distinctly remember her at the gate. I can still see her moving out of the gate, turning left, and walking past the scaly trunks of the fir trees that stood along the parapet wall between our garden and the gray asphalt road. I hear the sound of children coming from the school on the other side of the road—a continuing buzz like bees humming. It would have been late in the morning on a weekday.

I never saw Grandmother again.

A few days after she went through that wooden gate, painted blue and with a grill of the rising sun, a man was at the same gate calling.

"Is someone home?" That's how anyone would call when they came to that gate, and they had to call loud to be heard across the large front garden and through the veranda, the drawing room, and the dining room. Anyone who came to that gate and called from there also had to be someone coming for the first time and therefore didn't know it would not be opened unless under special circumstances. But that day it was opened. When Carolis, who had gone to see who it was at the gate, came running back looking frightened and told Mother there was a message from Kelaniya—now that was where Grandmother lived with her only son, the one who wore a red shawl and gave me a wooden car with a pedal—Mother wanted him to open the gate and let the man come. She stood on the edge of the veranda holding my hand.

The man came walking slowly along the left crescent of the driveway and stood under the portico.

Grandmother had died.

The day she left our place because she was offended by my giving her a bag to carry beef in, she had arrived home—meaning at her son's place where she lived—a couple of hours after high noon and, complaining of a headache, had gone to bed. She may have not had anything to eat since morning, because according to Mother, she didn't stay long enough at our place even to have a cup of tea. She had woken up after dark and taken a cold bath. Her daughter-in-law had warned her not to bathe at that time, but Grandmother never listened to anyone, least of all to her daughter-in-law. In the night she had a blazing temperature, and by morning she was in a delirium. Over the years something had nagged me in this whole affair. Had she been starving the whole day? Did anyone ask her whether she has had anything to eat? If she had been starving, why didn't she ask for something to eat? I have not been able to find this out, and there is this feeling within me that she starved herself to death. No one speaks about this, and it is like they want to avoid something. If she deliberately didn't eat anything, did it have something to do with what happened at our place, that stupid thing about my giving her a bag to carry beef in? I can't help but think that simple incident would have sparked off something that lay smoldering, something far more serious. I remember Mother telling Father, the night of the day Grandmother went through that front gate, that she insisted the gate be opened.

"I am not some vagrant to come and go through the back door. Why should I? I have a pedigree. My people were from the Maha Wasala. I am not a mixed-up half-caste." (By Maha Wasala, she meant the royal court of the Kandyan kings where Grandmother claimed her ancestors served; I don't know Grandmother's complete name, but she and her relatives—I have traced some of them now—lay claims to a family name that is of an illustrious highland clan, but I can't substantiate this. The reference to "half-caste" implies the hybridity of my father's side whose ancestry can be traced through their family name to Kerala, and they also have a Portuguese surname.)

As usual, Father had come home late in the night, and I was pretending to be fast asleep listening to Mother reporting the incident.

Now Grandmother was dead. The day after she developed high fever and became delirious, she was taken to hospital. She had died there sometime towards midnight, never once regaining consciousness. No final word, no dying wish.

But I knew nothing of all this until four years later.

The day the messenger came and Mother allowed him to come through the front gate, and he came slowly along the driveway, I was told that Grandmother was very ill. Mother kept crying because, I thought, she couldn't go see Grandmother, and that was because Father was not at home, and Mother couldn't leave without informing him, even if her mother was very ill. Father came home, as usual, late in the night.

The next morning Father took me in his red car with the long bonnet to that big house, from the veranda of which I could see the Spinning and Weaving Mills (Mother's brother, the one who made me a wooden car with a pedal, was no longer working there, having moved over to a factory that made safety matches and was situated at the north end of the city where he lived, and Grandmother lived with him, which is why she had to come in two trains whenever she came to see me) and the tall chimney smoking all the time. In that big house lived my father's only sister. She had no children at that time, and her husband was a doctor who worked in a provincial hospital far away. I was going to be with her for two days because my mother had to be with her mother, my grandmother who was very ill. Mother didn't come to drop me at the big house where my aunt lived. Mother never came to that house. I was unhappy going there. I was unhappy going anywhere without Mother. But I had to go. I began thinking of some of the interesting things at that big house. There was a piano on which Uncle Eugene played some strange melodies. Father told me that Uncle Neville, who lived in a wing at the back and had a car in which the hood could be dropped, was going to take me on a drive around the city. I had been to that house once before, and when there, I had seen a long line of horses moving along the road in front. The horses were beautiful to look at, moving rhythmically, their hooves making that clippity-clop sound, the swishing of the tails, and the proud way the heads were held. They were racehorses from Wallace's stables being taken for their morning exercises. This time when I was being taken to the big house I expected to see those horses again.

Uncle Neville didn't take me on that tour of the city. A little while after Father left me at the big house and went away, Uncle Neville left in his car that had a drop-head and didn't come back. Uncle Eugene was not at home. Perhaps he had gone to work. Even if he had been there, he would have hardly spoken with me. I began picking notes on the piano keyboard. It made a lovely sound. But my aunt asked me not to do that, because Uncle Eugene doesn't want anyone messing with the piano. It was his. So I sat in the long veranda. I could see the tall chimney and part of the roof of the Spinning and Weaving Mills through the coconut trees. A row of tenements ended on the other side of the road beyond the gate of the big house I was in. Where it ended there was a laundry with a serving counter opening on to the road. As the day moved towards high noon there was a blue haze like a thin smoke on the fronds of the coconut palms. There was no wind, and the air became hot. My eyes hurt, and I wanted to be back home standing at the bay window of the upper level and looking over the green tree-tops at the back garden to the rice paddies with the sun on them and perhaps, if it was a clear day, to the blue hills beyond where the Holy Peak would stand sharp and clear and still like a picture, and down below at the courtyard Mother would be fussing, feigning anger with the servant women, quick in movement, and the wood smoke coming out of the kitchen hanging lightly over the passion fruit creeper carrying warm smells of food cooking over slowly burning fires.

A huge booming, bellowing sound rolled over everything and stopped. It was the siren at the mills blowing the work shift, and it frightened me. I may have heard it this close before, but this was the first time in my memory. That fear was there long after the sound had stopped, and then the horses appeared. I ran down the steps and along the drive, all the way up to the gate. Watching those magnificent animals from behind the gate was not enough for me. I opened the gate slightly and stood outside by the edge of the road, where I could almost touch the animals. Their flanks rippled as they moved and they snorted, spraying white flecks of foam from their mouths. There was a man with each animal holding it by the muzzle. The men were Tamils, charcoal black and wiry, wearing white turbans, which made them look darker. The horses exuded a strong musky odor that, for me, was not unpleasant, and I held on to it for days like something I enjoyed. The long line of horses stretched all the way up the road, and the first ones were already past the gate I was standing at, but I began counting from there. I had counted twelve when I heard a voice behind me. It was calling for me but not addressing me by my name or in any other way. It just kept saying "Here! Here!" in a high-pitched irritated manner. I looked back, and through the half-open gate I saw Barnis, the manservant at the big house come running along the drive. Barnis was a freak. He was very short, and his face was like it had been smashed up and hurriedly reassembled with everything in the wrong place. Now he was angry, and that made him look more weird. He grabbed me by the hand and pulled me violently inside and closed the gate. He did all this at the same time — or so I felt — and he was trying to say something, none of which I could understand. But I vaguely felt that I had done something terribly wrong, but what was wrong about me standing outside the gate watching a row of horses moving along the road their shining flanks rippling their tails swishing their hooves clippity-clopping and the Tamil horse-keepers in their white turbans looking black as charcoal' and a musky odor heavy in the air, was something I couldn't understand. But here was Barnis the freak, with his face like it had been taken apart and put back together all wrong, taking me by the hand towards the portico of the big house where, on the steps leading up to the veranda, stood my aunt, arms akimbo and looking very angry indeed. For sometime — that is until Barnis the freak came and said lunch was ready — my aunt and I stood in the veranda repeating two different things over and over again. She kept saying that where those tenements were on the other side of the road was a very bad place where bad people lived, and that decent people had nothing to do with them, looking the other way when passing the row of houses; the inmates of those houses were not allowed to come within the compound of this big house, and there had been a time until recently when those wretched people would not carry an umbrella over their heads going past the front gate. All this meant nothing to me, and I kept saying that I had gone out merely to see the horses, but she kept saying the same thing over and over again. There was a fear in her voice like I had done something very dangerous and had been rescued in the nick of time. Whenever I am here, she warned, that fear still lurking in her eyes and her voice, I should not go out by myself; if any of those bad people living in those tenements spoke with me, I was to remain silent, and if they smiled, I was not to return the smile. She made the whole thing sound very serious, as if I violated any of those rules something terrible was going to happen. Then came Barnis the freak to say lunch was ready, and he looked like he had done his good deed for the day by finding me at the gate and bringing me back.

Lunch was like being at a prayer. Aunt sat at the head of the table and I sat on her right and there was total silence. Barnis the freak hovered in the background. I began to hate him. I felt my aunt's eyes on me, which made me uneasy, and I kept looking away from the food. The walls reached very high to a carved wooden ceiling. On the walls were large portraits of men and women in elaborate ceremonial dress, and the frames were very ornate, and some had gilt edges. In front of me, and kept against the wall, was a large chiffonier, and its mirror was framed by a grapevine with bunches at regular intervals carved into the ebony wood. I saw myself reflected in the mirror, and just behind me, standing like an evil spirit, was Barnis.

That monstrous sound like the bellowing of a dying beast rolled over everything once again, and I woke up and wanted to scream. It was like not being able to open my eyes, and I was shaking all over. Slowly I realized it was night, and that I was somewhere in that big house with those high walls going up to the carved ceiling. I had sat up in bed, and now I could see a faint glow through the open door of the room I was in. It was a dim light in the dining hall, and I was in a room opening out into that hall, and I could see the mirror of the chiffonier there, a rectangle of muted reflection. I laid back on the bed, where the bedsheet and the pillowcase felt like crisp paper and smelled of laundry-starch. I now remembered Aunt preparing this bed, and the fear I had of having to sleep there all alone because I had never slept alone, and Aunt not even asking me whether it would be all right by me if I was to sleep alone. At the time she left me there and disappeared, the lights were still on in the house, and Uncle Eugene was playing the piano, and it was a beautiful sound, rather sad, and I felt good. I heard cars on the lane going by the side of the house, and all the cars seemed like they were coming home. Dogs barked, some far away and some not so far away, but they never barked altogether like they did in the village where my home was, and the sounds were different. These were deep pedigreed barks, arrogant and full of assurance, not sounds of fear, pain or appeal.

The piano had stopped. It may have stopped when I was listening to the dogs. I first heard the silence like some emptiness. Then the lights began to go out one by one. I heard the click of the switches putting out the lights. It must have been Barnis the freak. Once all the lights were off and the clicking of the switches stopped, it was dark except for a vague light that fell across the dining room. From the bed on which I lay, I could see that light through an open door. That's when I began getting frightened. I did not know from where that light was coming, and it cast shadows on the wall. The mirror of the chiffonier reflected a corner of the dining room, and there were certain dark shapes there. I shut my eyes and began crying into the pillow. I tried to cry softly without making a sound, and that gave me a pain inside me like my chest was going to burst.

Waves crashed on the beach and sea gulls squawked and Grandmother was with me but constantly running away, and her face was a blank, and I couldn't run, and there was a pain in my chest like I couldn't breathe. It was then that the dying monster howled, and I woke up and sat on bed shaking all over and then saw the vague light in the hall beyond the open door and the muted reflection of the mirror on the chiffonier in the dining room and realized I was at the big house where lived my aunt and that freak Barnis, and the sound like a dying monster's was really the siren at the mill. As I lay back in bed, there was a huge silence, as if the sound of the siren had created a vacuum. As I shut my eyes again, I was listening to that silence, wanting to hear some sound, and through that dark and the awesome stillness I began to hear something. At first it was like part of the silence, and the sound I thought I heard was like a humming in the ears when you cupped it with your hands. It rose and fell, and then I recognized it, and it was like someone held your hand and you were not frightened anymore. It was the sound of the sea. The sea was about a mile away from the big house I was now in, but you never heard it during the day. Now in the still of the night, and after the siren seemed to have blown away everything and cleared the air, you heard the waves crashing on the beach. I knew that sound well by then. I first heard it when I was with Grandmother in a house somewhere off the south coast where Father had a rubber plantation, and once he took us there to stay for some time. That was the only time that Grandmother was with us like part of the family, and Mother made me sleep with Grandmother in another room, and I liked it because she—Grandmother—told me wonderful stories and held me close when we slept, and it was nice and warm and pleasant holding on to her and sleeping.

We arrived at the rubber plantation one morning—I remember it was morning because I woke up in the car where I would have been put while still in my sleep, feeling hungry, and Mother said we were going to have breakfast at the estate bungalow, and sure enough there was a feast of hoppers, the best I have eaten so far, awaiting us, and immediately after breakfast I went for a walk with Grandmother. Mother wanted us to go until she arranged things at the bungalow. We walked under the rubber trees, and it was cool, and the thick carpet of dead leaves was still wet with overnight dew, and there was a strong smell of latex mixed with decaying leaves, and Grandmother picked rubber seeds on the ground—brown-shelled and brittle, enclosed in two ear-shaped clasps. Grandmother showed me how to separate the clasps and reconnect them in a different way, and when you blew on one, it made a whirring sound as it spun like a bobbin. There were women collecting latex in galvanized buckets, and they paused to look at us, smiling diffidently at first, and when Grandmother spoke with them they grinned from ear to ear, and some of them touched me on the head. We kept walking, me blowing at those bobbins until my mouth was dry, and the ground began to rise, and then we were clear of the rubber trees and above them on an open expanse of flat rock, and suddenly I heard Grandmother's voice excited like a child's.

"There's the sea."

I looked, and it took some time for me to see what Grandmother saw. It was a sheer expanse of emerald green touching the blue dome of the sky at the far end in a wide crescent, and on the land side, where the green tops of coconut trees ended on a gold-colored strip, there were what looked like white plumes forever appearing and disappearing. There were boats all over on the green water, and they were bobbing with their sails bright in the eastern sun. A strong wind was blowing from the sea, and it was heavy unlike the winds that blew across the paddy fields at home. Grandmother kept explaining all of this to me, and I can still hear the sense of wonder in her voice. She called what we were looking at—that great big spread of green water touching the blue sky with those milky-white plumes at the land's edge—the Moaning Pond. That's what her people up in the hills called the sea. Because, she said, the sea always keeps making that sound—here she imitated the sea-sound—like a woman is moaning. When she was a little girl, very few people up there in her village had seen the Moaning Pond, and those who had were held in great respect. She herself had never seen it until she came down to the lowlands with her husband. However, once when she was a little girl she had gone on a pilgrimage to the Holy Peak, and there at the summit at daybreak, when the sun rose from the east and cast the peak's shadow across the land, people with her had pointed in the distance and said if you keep looking hard you will see the Moaning Pond. She kept looking hard and for a long time, she said, and thought she saw something shimmering at a faraway point where the shadow of the peak seemed to end. But she was not sure. Ever since that day, she wanted to see the Moaning Pond and dip her feet in its salty wash, which was almost a necessary ritual for those who come there for the first time. They called it "walking the waves." Waves were those things like white plumes, and they keep dashing on the beach. The beach is that strip of gold-colored ground. That's all sand. Fine white sand. There are shells of various colors to be picked up in the sand. Bathing in the sea was good. It cured you of many ailments and made you healthy. The sea, in the way Grandmother described it, was a marvel, something that began nowhere and ended nowhere. A great big mysterious pond, which kept moaning eternally, like a woman in anguish. She dashes herself on the shore all the time. Associated with the waves breaking on the shore, I have always carried with me this image of a woman throwing herself on the ground weeping, because that's how Grandmother first described it to me. She didn't say it directly, but her choice of words implied that image. For her, waves did not break on the shore, they threw themselves, and the word she used is a verb in our language that connotes an act of penance, and when she first said that on that rock above the rubber trees looking towards the sea, her voice, as I have always remembered, was very sad.

That night, when I slept with Grandmother, snuggled comfortably to her warmth, we listened to the sound of the sea, now coming from far away. I drifted away to sleep listening to that sound, but before that, until sleep came, Grandmother told me the first of many stories connected with the sea I was to hear in the days to come.

Once-upon-a-time the sea became very angry, because a wicked king who ruled in Kelaniya—now that's at the mouth of the great river that flows through that valley along the slopes of which Grandmother descended from the hills with that disrobed Buddhist monk wearing a turban to hide his shaven head and whose village was on the edge of the rice paddies snaking around innumerable ridges all the way to the sea—burnt to death ninety Buddhist monks. They were put inside cauldrons of boiling oil. The sea reared furiously in shock and anger, and great big waves like mountains crashed upon the city wreaking death and destruction. Astrologers were called, and the King was advised that the sea to be appeased demands a human sacrifice, a young girl. Now the King had an only child, a delicate princess of great beauty. And she very bravely offered herself to be the sacrifice, so that her father's kingdom may be saved from the wrath of the sea. On a boat made of gold and decked with flowers and amidst the wailing and weeping of the people, the beautiful Princess was set sail on the angry waves. But she did not drown. The sea carried her gently on its waves all the way to the deep south of the island and deposited her safely on the shores of another kingdom. The King there recognized the girl to be a princess and took her as his queen. In due course this queen bore him two sons, one of whom became a great warrior who, at the head of a great army, reconquered for us our traditional homeland in the north-central plains known as Raja Rata—or the King's Country—from a foreign invader who had occupied it for four-and-a-half decades.

The next morning, Father took us to the sea beach. It would

have been the monsoon season because the sea was rough and tall waves crashed on the shore—wailing women throwing themselves in penance—and my mind was full of concern for that beautiful princess who was put out to sea as a sacrifice. In my mind it was like she was still out there tossing perilously on those angry waves in her golden boat. Mother wouldn't let me go near the waves, but Grandmother was at the water's edge "walking the waves," and she seemed as happy as a child. That's another memory of Grandmother that I carry with me—dressed in white playing like a child by the sea, the white foam of the waves rising up to her, and she not running back but standing there, very still as if in some secret communion.

That's the image of Grandmother that came back to me when I heard the sound of the sea coming from far away on that lonely night in the big house where Father had left me with his sister, my aunt, and I had woken in the night to the fearful cry of a dying monster. Now with the sound of the sea floating gently up to me from somewhere, it was like being with Grandmother, and I almost felt her warmth, and the room filled with the strong-sweet smell of betel, cardamom and perfumed oil, and I was not frightened anymore.

I began speaking with Grandmother. I told her I was sorry she was ill, that I hoped she would be all right soon and that she would come to see me; maybe Father would take us to that bungalow in the rubber estate again and we would—Grandmother and I—walk under those rubber trees on the dead leaves wet with dew, blowing that bobbin made of those ear-shaped clasps until my mouth was all dry, and that we would walk all the way up to that rock from where we would watch the Moaning Pond in the distance. I also told her I was sorry if I hurt her with that fool talk of the leather bag for her to carry beef in, that I didn't intend to hurt her because I loved her more than anything else in the world.

"How's Grandmother?"

"She's all right."

Mother wasn't looking at me straight.

"Can I go see her?"

"No you can't."

"Why?"

"She's gone away to the hills."

"Why?"

"Because it's cool up there and she would get better soon."

"Can't we go up there to see her?"

"Not yet."

"How long will she be up there?"

"Until she gets completely well."

"Then will she come back?"

"Yes."

"And then will she come to see me?"

"Yes."

"If she doesn't come can we go see her?"

"Yes."

Mother was feeding me at the table. Father had just brought me back from the big house where his sister lived. Father too was at the table. He was eating. Right through this conversation he kept eating silently, his eyes fixed continuously on his plate.

Three years pass, and I am still waiting for Grandmother to return from the hills, when Doreen and Felicia came to stay with us. They were sisters, and their mother had died—or so I was told, but I think it was something else—and their father, who was a friend of my father's, wanted them to stay with us until he made some other permanent arrangements. Doreen and Felicia were older than I—I was going on eight—and I knew they were older because they had boobs. Not big ones, but boobs nevertheless. We soon became very friendly, and among the things I told them about myself was that I had a grandmother and that she was up in the hills where it was cool and where she had gone to get well and that she would be coming back one day soon. Doreen and Felicia looked at each other and didn't say anything.

The two sisters went to school in the morning. Their school was somewhere in Colombo, and they traveled by train. I still wasn't going to school, though I was big enough to be going — and that's another story. When they came back from school, Doreen and Felicia would be inside their room until Mother called them out for tea, which was late in the afternoon. The girls occupied a room that was at the end of a long corridor leading away from the dining hall. When you are in that room it was like being away from the rest of the house. It had two windows that looked out to a lonely part of the garden on a side of the house full of large trees, where it was always sunless and gloomy. There was a door, other than the one from which you entered the room, at the end of the corridor. This door would open into the left corner of the front garden, but it was permanently locked. A large iron bed and an old wardrobe with a mirror on one door — the mirror had gray patches where the mercury had faded — was all the furniture in that room, and there was a large framed monochrome picture — I am not certain now whether it was a painting or a photograph — of a reclining woman. She had frizzy hair and wore a strange dress. On the border, at the bottom between the frame and the picture, was a legend printed in letters that stretched and curved and leaned in fancy curlicues which said "A Maori Girl."

The time that Doreen and Felicia were inside the room after coming back from school was the time Mother had her afternoon nap, and the servants would be downstairs unseen and unheard, and everything was still and silent, and I had nothing to do. Sleep wouldn't come to me at that time, and normally I was in bed with Mother, waiting for her to wake up. That was until a week or so after Doreen and Felicia came to stay with us.

Then I began to be with them inside their room with the door closed. At first we lay in bed talking. I was in the middle of that iron bed with the two girls on either side of me. That was the time I told them about my grandmother being in the hills getting well and also many other things. Some of what I said was true, but most of the time I was inventing stories, like the one about my going out to sea in a boat when the sea came right up to our veranda at the bungalow on that rubber estate. The girls used to hug me and caress me, and I didn't mind. It was like being with Grandmother. One day Doreen slid her hand down to my waist and then underneath my trouser and began fondling my wee-wee, and at first I wriggled and squirmed, but then Felicia held me by my hands, and slowly I became still because it was pleasant in a way I had not felt before. Very soon I began to wait for them to come back from school and to be with them inside their room, and we were getting on to more interesting things, like they would lift their frocks and remove their knickers—those loose, puffed shorts reaching halfway down the thighs that girls wore underneath their frocks—and I could see a very vague growth of hair in a triangle just above where their thighs ended, and then we began playing "Doctors and Patients," where I had to lie down and let them remove my trousers completely, and they would each take turns fondling my wee-wee, and it was very pleasant, and then it was my turn to examine them in turns, and I had to touch below that vague triangle of hair as each one lay in bed with their knickers pulled down and eyes closed.

This didn't last too long. One day when Felicia was the "patient" in bed, and I was doing to her what I am supposed to do as the "doctor," the doors to the room flew open with a sound like it had been pushed violently from the outside, and Mother stood there looking like nothing I had seen her look like before.

Two days later Doreen and Felicia were gone. I didn't see them go. I never saw them after that day when Mother burst into the room. It was not that I was prevented from seeing them. But I avoided seeing them, and they would have done the same. Mother kept me with her all the time. She never asked me about what I was doing inside the room with Doreen and Felicia. But I knew she was angry. Whether she was angry with me or with the two girls, it was difficult to say.

After Doreen and Felicia left there was something I wanted to ask Mother. They left in the morning, and I spent a long time making up my mind to ask what I wanted to ask Mother. It was late in the afternoon, and through the bay windows in the upper level I could see the light dying on the rice paddies beyond the treetops. The blue hills in the distance had vanished in a gray sky, and there was a hint of rain in the wind that blew over the trees right inside the house. Seated on that easy chair where long ago Grandmother sat on the day she went through the front gate never to return, Mother was reading a book. She always sat there when she read something, because at those windows the light was there long after it had gone from the rest of the house.

"Mother!"

She didn't look up from the book she was reading but made a sound like she heard me.

"Is Grandmother dead?"

Now she looked up. She seemed surprised. I am sure she would have detected the complaint in my voice. I had waited for this moment, since Doreen and Felicia told me that Grandmother was dead and that this story about her being in the hills was a big lie. But they swore me to say I wouldn't say that they told me so. Now that Doreen and Felicia were gone, I was free to ask.

"Who told you?"

"Tell me, is she dead?"

Mother took a long time—or it seemed to me—to answer. She looked down at the book then looked away through the window to the dark coming under the trees in the back garden down below. I heard the whistle of the Little Train before I heard Mother answer me at last.

"Yes."

For a moment I was silent. I felt something building up within me, slowly. At first I began sobbing, and Mother reached out like she wanted to touch me. I screamed as loud as I had ever done. Mother stood up like she was struck by something. I tore into her, screaming all the time. By the time the servants came running, I had my teeth into Mother's hand. I wouldn't let anyone touch me, and I rolled on the ground and then stood up again screaming still, looking around for things to throw at those who kept reaching for me. I now remember that there came a point when I couldn't stop myself thrashing around. I wasn't doing it only because I had not been told that Grandmother was dead. That was only one reason. I felt cheated like your getting hurt when you are made a fool of. There was something more. I think it had much to do with Mother bursting into the room when I was playing "doctor" with Felicia, the "patient," lying in bed with her frock raised and the knickers down. At that moment, something stopped within me, and I became still and stood where I stood when Mother took me by the hand and led me out of the room. She didn't say a word, and for two days something was choked up within me. What made it worse was that everyone was behaving strangely with me. Alice, the servant woman who would bathe me and dress me, had a funny look when she changed my clothes, and I was feeling uneasy. There was a silence whenever people moved past me or they were in my presence. It was like some horrible thing had happened, something that should not be spoken about. What was choked within me perhaps was shame. During those two days between Mother bursting into the room and Doreen and Felicia going away, I didn't want to talk to anyone. Guilt was a feeling unknown to me then, I suppose. But death, I was vaguely aware of. People who die never come back. When Doreen—and Felicia too was there—first told me that Grandmother was dead, and that she would never come back—that was many days before they had to go from our house—I was not sad immediately. I was angry. First I was angry with the two girls because I thought they were lying. Then over the next few days when I began to realize that maybe it was true, I was angry with Mother. Then when I went to sleep in the night, and lying in bed next to the bed where Mother was sleeping, I began to think of Grandmother. I listened to the night, and I thought I heard the sound of the Moaning Pond come from far away, and then the room would be filled with the sweet-strong smell of betel and cardamom and perfumed oil, and tears would come. I cried softly not to wake up Mother, because if she woke up I would have to explain why I was crying and that would be bad because I had promised Doreen and Felicia I wouldn't tell Mother that they told me Grandmother was dead.

However, when Doreen and Felicia went away, and I asked my Mother whether Grandmother was really dead and she said "yes," and I screamed and yelled and thrashed on the floor, it was not only that I was sad Grandmother was dead.

I had been doing something horrible with Doreen and Felicia inside their room.

Everyone's looking at me in a funny sort of way because of that.

Doreen and Felicia have been sent away.
There's something choking inside me.
Grandmother isn't in the hills getting well.
They have lied to me all these years.
I have been cheated.
Grandmother was dead.
Really dead.
Dead.
All of this was there in my scream, in the way I tore into Mother, thrashed on the floor and looked for things to throw at those who were trying to reach out and calm me.

I screamed all those things and many other things I couldn't say with words.

It was also the end of something. The screaming and the rolling on the floor and the biting of Mother's hand and the rushing at people who tried to touch me like a yapping snarling dog were the death throes of something that died that day. Whatever it was, it died hard like a grievously wounded animal struggling and thrashing around until the last breath was drawn.

After the coming and going of Doreen and Felicia, life somehow became different. A new shame had entered me, and I had things to hide, things I would see that I had not seen before and I would not talk about.

There were also other things that changed. A year after Doreen and Felicia left, we moved from the split-level house with the bay windows to a smaller one in the same neighborhood. The servants left one by one, and only Carolis remained. The red car with the long bonnet was gone. Father came and went in a small Bug Fiat, and one day he kept it behind in the portico — small though the house was, it had a portico with an unpaved floor that was full of dust — and it remained there for a long time until someone came and towed it away and it never came back. Things were going away never to come back like Grandmother. Only Tony, my roly-poly-fluffy pup, now grown lean and tall with the puppy fat gone, remained, and it was fun going around with him under the rubber trees across the paddy field at the edge of the compound and collecting fish from the little streams into empty Horlicks bottles. Grandmother was dead, and when I went to sleep alone in my room next to my parents' room with a communicating door, I did not hear the Moaning Pond anymore, and I didn't seem to care.

When I began going to the movies, the Moaning Pond was always there behind the Savoy theater, and very near the Majestic, and not so near yet visible in the distance from the front of the Liberty. Sometimes after a show I would walk with my friend Wicky along the rail tracks that went just above the beach where, on the rocks, couples would be huddled under black umbrellas and the waves thrashed on the shore—the wailing women—and Grandmother was never there in my thoughts.

The tilted peak of Hunnasgiriya—The Misty Mountain—so called because it is wreathed in mist at all times of the day— appeared and disappeared through the thick foliage covering the rising-falling land through which Asanka and I were walking along a narrow gravel path that dipped and then rose all the way to the river bank. It was still early in the day, and we were taking our morning walk. It had nothing to do with keeping healthy. We were just happy in each other's company, and walked holding hands, and we could have gone walking like that forever.

At forty I had walked out of an unhappy marriage and my job as a film director at the Government Film Unit and, packing some clothes and a part of my collection of books into a battered T-Model Ford, had driven one hundred kilometers to Kandy, where a friend had found me half a house to live in. Asanka joined me a week later. She was twenty-two and the eldest in a regular churchgoing orthodox Methodist family and had to run away to be with me. The house we lived in overlooked a narrow strip of rice paddy with steep embankments on either side, along which ran two gravel paths through bush and shrub and, intermittently, tall flamboyant trees always red with blossoms, all the way to the right bank of the Mahaweli River. If you turned left and walked along the high river bank for some time you came to a beautiful railway bridge like the ones you see in paintings with graceful arches—built by the British over one hundred and twenty years ago—that crossed the river. There was a little passage between the steel girders for pedestrians on the bridge, and if you walk along that you reached a little town—Katugastota—The Ferry of the Thorn Trees. If you took a right turn at the end of either of those gravel paths that ran along the embankments on either side of the paddy field, you walked along lovely woodland—large trees with big canopies, green grass permanently dew-wet with the river flowing on your left at almost the same level—until you came to a spot called Paranagamtota—The Old Ferry—where, in 1802, a British regiment, retreating from Kandy after an abortive invasion, was slaughtered, except for one man who, according to his diary written later in London, swam across the river holding with one hand his partly severed head, and he also had a pellet sticking out of his nose, permanently embedded there, which made him something of an exhibit back home. The river is broad here, because this is where it begins to leave the hills after flowing all the way through mountains from the eastern side of the Holy Peak, to flow out in a series of slow drops in the land to the eastern plains.

Asanka and I would walk right along the river bank, and at

the Old Ferry would turn away from the river and begin a series of climbs that brought us to a good asphalt road that came down from the hills to another section of the rail track that ran somewhere above where we lived. Coming down from the rail track we would be back home before the sun touched the treetops and it began to get hot, and the people were out on the roads, and we couldn't hold hands.

It was on these walks that I suddenly found myself talking about Grandmother once again after many years. Things long forgotten came back into memory, and I must have begun weaving them into a story, connecting the dots, to make it interesting. That is the story I have written here about Grandmother in the way I recalled it during those long walks with Asanka, with the river flowing gently and the tilted peak looming beyond in the slowly brightening sky. The young girl, nearly half my age holding on to my hand, so trusting and so vulnerable, may have reminded me of Grandmother leaving her home in the hills at sixteen and going away with a man to an unknown future from which she never came back. Her village was somewhere across the river at the foot of that mountain with a tilted peak — if what I had heard about her origins was true. If so, the temple where my grandfather was a young Buddhist priest before he disrobed himself to run away with a sixteen-year-old girl, should also be there. I knew the name of the village. It was the name of the clan my Grandmother's people claimed their descent from, and all Kandyan clans used the name of the village of their origin.

A month after Asanka and I came to live in a part of that house that overlooked the narrow strip of paddy stretching all the way to the river, we had the whole house to ourselves because the owner, an old bachelor who lived in the other part, left the country for some personal reason. It was a large but homely cottage, of which every corner was bright and sunlit with the wind from the river coming across the rice paddies and moving through the house at all times of the day.

The money I had—I had withdrawn a greater part of my bank balance before leaving Colombo—was enough for three months, but that was a long time ahead. We lived in the moment through those long walks in the early mornings, and in the late afternoons strolling the streets of the city just below its lake, and sometimes seated for hours on the scalloped wall surrounding the Palace of the Tooth, watching the comings and goings of white-clad devotees, and the drums began to beat and the pipes began to blow and the night came slowly down the timbered hills all around. Grandmother was there all the time, up front or right behind.

It was then that I began to question myself. Why did I come here? My decision to abandon all that I had grown up with, turn my back on family, job, and social security, and the cheerful indifference to the big scandal that followed my act, could easily have been realized elsewhere. Kandy provided no special security from the wrath of those whom both of us had left behind or walked out on, to be with each other. Kandy was my choice of sanctuary. Why? Was it some secret longing for a place that memory recalls as it does in migrant birds?

Some mornings I would linger a little at the Old Ferry before beginning to climb the rising land to turn back home. I wanted to see somewhere in my mind that terrible scene when the English regiment and the Malay and Kaffir mercenaries were slaughtered. Records say it had been raining heavily, and the river was in spate. I met a very old man whose father had been a ferryman there. He claims that even now the place was haunted. On rainy nights during the monsoon storms he had heard the moans and screams of dying soldiers. The massacre took place on 28 June 1803. I began calculating in my mind. Grandmother was sixty-five when she died. That was in 1944.

She was sixteen when she left her village in the hills somewhere within two miles of this place. That would have been in 1895. At sixteen she would have known people who, in turn, would have known people who were alive during the Massacre at the Old Ferry, which had now become myth and legend. How sad Grandmother had to die so early before I could get more information about her past. My uncle, the one who built me a wooden car with a pedal, too was gone. My mother knew very little. Grandmother hardly spoke of her childhood, says Mother. My aunt, the one who is now like a child, crying and smiling in turn, can't even remember the coming to Colombo — a trip which, once again according to family legend, was by boat through the night along a series of waterways that brought timber and plumbago from the western slopes to the city.

That was the longing, the seeking of a bloodline to a past my grandmother came from. Ten years short of a hundred after Grandmother left the hills, a sixteen-year-old girl going away to the edge of the land where the Moaning Pond lay, turning her back on everything she belonged to, a part of her had returned, this time as a man with a girl by his side.

That is the story I want to tell. It is the story that began to grow in me during those days in the hills with Asanka, when after a long time I was happy once again. My last happy days before that were when I was still waiting for Grandmother to return from the hills, and I was in that split-level house with the bay windows through which I could see the light on the rice paddies, and beyond that on clear days the blue mountains in the distance. All that ended the day I asked Mother whether Grandmother was dead because Doreen and Felicia had told me so and had asked me not to wait for her because dead people don't come back, and when Mother said "yes," I screamed and tore into Mother, bit her hand, rolled on the floor, and got up again looking around for things to throw at everyone who was trying to reach out to me. I can't say I became unhappy because I came to know that Grandmother was dead and would not come back. There were many other things that made life unpleasant—now that's another story. But since that day, life was bad for me until I drove all the way in a battered T-Model Ford to Kandy, and Asanka joined me a week later to live together in a house overlooking a narrow strip of rice paddy that stretched right up to the river, and we began walking early in the mornings holding hands with the tilted peak of Hunnas-giriya—The Misty Mountain—looming in the background.

If in me Grandmother returned to the hills that she left behind, the story had come full circle, and I wanted to be where the story began ten-less-than-a-hundred years ago.

The way was steep, paved with pieces of splintered rock placed irregularly. The paved rocks were worn smooth and looked like they have been trod for hundreds of years. But today, as I was moving up slowly, almost step by step, I met no one. There were temple trees lining the route on both sides, and they were full of flowers, white and red, scenting the cool morning air. The pathway was covered with fallen flowers, and the wet petals made it slippery on the smooth rocks. I sat on the edge of a flat rocky surface where there was a depression scooped in, to hold oil perhaps, I thought. I had seen a few more such rocks on the way up. Seated on the rock I looked up and saw no end of the climb. The pathway turned left abruptly, a little further up, and disappeared. On either side the wood was thick, and you couldn't look too far. It was like walking through a tunnel. I wondered whether I had come to the right place. I had no clues except for a picture in my mind. How that picture came to be there, I was not sure. It had been there for a long time. Unlike the story of Grandmother that I had pieced together like connecting the dots, this picture of a temple on a rock had been there always with all the details. I could not remember its beginning. It was like a place I had been to, something I had seen for real. But the climb along the rock-paved path, with the temple trees lining both sides and the flowers fallen thick on the ground, wasn't part of the picture. That was the reason for the pause, the sitting down on the rock with a flat surface on which was a depression scooped for oil, and the doubt in my mind whether I am in the right place. It was the old man at the Old Ferry, whose father had been a ferryman and who still hears the cries of the dying British soldiers of the massacre on rainy nights, who directed me to this temple I was climbing to. I had described to him the picture in my mind and the village where this temple should be. He knew the village very well; it was a half-hour's drive along the main road that crossed the river parallel to the railway bridge. There were two temples in that village, and one was exactly as I had described.

The asphalt road climbed for more than four miles and then nose-dived to a valley of terraced paddy, and I was in the village now from which I believed Grandmother came, and to which she never returned. I had left Asanka behind because I wanted to be alone. It was a very private affair, but more than that there was this uneasy feeling I was doing something silly, and when you did something like that you wanted to be alone.

Around me were hills rising sheer from the floor of the valley, and the skyline was a rim, and you felt you were at the bottom of a huge crater. I was on the eastern edge of the old Kingdom, and if you climbed out of this crater towards where the sun was now moving you would see the rolling Dumbara Hills—renamed Knuckles by the British planters and big game hunters—a great stairway going down to the edge of the land where lay Grandmother's Moaning Pond.

Following the instructions of the old man at the Old Ferry, I turned into a gravel path that moved across the rice paddies, rising tier upon tier, and the road forever climbing and the men and women transplanting ankle deep in water and mud glinting in the angled morning sun, and they standing up to look at my car—the single ugly object where everything else was natural and beautiful and blended in graceful harmony—and the men could not be told from the women because their heads were covered with cloth of various colors, and I stop at an ambalama—the old resting places for travelers found mostly in the middle of vast paddy fields in the old Kingdom because it was along the paddy fields that people walked from one village to another and over long distances—and I park the car there, lock it up, and begin my trek to that temple in my mind which, if the old man at the Old Ferry was right, should be at the rim of the crater at a spot straight up in front of where I was now.

That's how I was seated on a rock after having left the paddy field behind me with my car parked near the traveler's rest and walking through a wooded hillside and climbing a path paved with rocks worn smooth by feet over centuries and now slippery with fallen flowers from the temple trees, heavy with red and white blossoms.

The climb is resumed, and at the abrupt turn of the rock-paved pathway to the left, the temple trees are no more, and the land falls away steeply on either side where no tree could grow. I was now on a narrow ridge not wide enough for two people to pass, and it moves level up to the foot of a flight of steps leading up once more to where I could see, through the thick green foliage, something white. Leaving the narrow ridge behind, I climb the steps cut into a rock, and the white I saw through the trees now becomes a part of the temple, one wall of a rectangular building standing on thick columns of timber and crossbeams. The roof is hipped, and the valance is laced with pendant tiles. The bare face of the white wall is broken by two small windows and a narrow door in the middle, all closed. The wall is not quite white; it has a tinge of vague blue, but the light falling clear from the sky gives the wall a fierce white glare, and I take time to adjust my vision. The hard light was on the front wall and over the flat-tiled hipped roof and lay beyond the building where there was a break in the thick green foliage. On the right end of the building there was an open space of clean white sand going all the way to a rocky bluff, rising in boulders to a height where I could see the canopy of a Bo tree. All this was awash in that hard light where everything looked sharp and clearly defined. At the top of the steps that I had climbed and now stood, I was in shade, and it was cool and comfortable there. The contrast between the shade in which I stood and the hard light beyond was very sharp. I had climbed from the west, and now I was facing the sun. I had a feeling I had come from behind to the temple premises, and the main entrance should be on the other side where the sunlight was. Perhaps that was why this still looked different to the picture in my mind. I was seeing it from a different angle.

I sat on the edge of a low brick wall that ran along the edge of the compound, both ways from the end of the stone steps, and began removing my shoes. I had worn lacing shoes with socks underneath. You never wear those to temple, because it is messy removing them, and more messy putting them on again with all the sand that gets into your soles. I took time unlacing the shoes, removing the socks, and putting them carefully inside the shoes. All the time I kept looking down, and when I looked up a priest was standing there. He was in that hard light beyond the side of the building and stood quite still. From the shade I walked into the sun, and moving up to the priest I knelt down and worshipped him, and he murmured the usual blessing. His voice was faint and indifferent. I noticed he had peasant's feet, rough and coarse, and his robe was dirty at the hem. When I stood up, he kept looking at me silently for some time, and his face was very hard and unfriendly. He was waiting for me to talk. I said I was passing by and wanted to come up and have a look.

"Passing by going where?" I knew I was getting into a difficult situation.

"I was going along the road down there." I said pointing vaguely towards where I came from.

"But that road goes nowhere."

"I was going to that village at the end of the road."

"You know someone there?"

"No. But I wanted to have a look."

"Any particular reason?"

"It's a famous village."

"Yes. Many famous people bear the name of that village. But none of them were born here. Their ancestors left the village and made good elsewhere. No one came back. No one who leaves ever comes back. Not even the Bhikkhus, who go for higher education from this temple." There was bitterness in his voice.

"Only the poor remain."

I wanted to confide in him. Speak the truth and say why I was here. But I wasn't sure of anything anymore. Yet there was that temple in my mind. It was like some origin myth both true and untrue.

Suddenly the priest wanted to know from where I came.

"From where are you?" This question in my language implies much more than your place of residence. It wants to know your origin. I didn't want to say I was from Colombo. I said I was from Kandy. That was a mistake. The priest's eyes brightened. He wanted me to be more specific, and when I answered truthfully came the fatal question. My name? I answered. His face darkened.

"You can't be from up here." "Up here" meant the Old Kingdom. No. He began walking away from me, and I followed. I felt he expected me to follow him. Was he leading me somewhere? He stopped at the end of the sand-strewn compound where the boulders were, rising from one to the other to the spot where the Bo tree was. No one else could be seen around. The compound had not been swept in days. The place looked neglected.

"There are some old paintings in the shrine room." He pointed to that building with the hipped roof and the valance with pendant tiles that I had come by.

"You may go up to the Bo tree and offer some flowers. I'll have the shrine room opened for you." I watched him move away towards the priest's quarters, which was at the end of another rectangular space between the shrine room and the boulders. It was like a courtyard and there were temple trees. The priest was walking under those trees, and he looked very tall.

The path to the Bo tree avoided the boulders and moved up in a spiral. As I was reaching the top, I felt a cold breeze. It was typical tea-country wind, and to my right, over the Dumbara Hills, I saw the distant range of peaks where the plantations were.

The Bo Maluwa—Compound of the Bo Tree—was on the edge of the rise where the land fell sharply through timbered hillsides to terraced fields of rice paddy, where the sun lay in bright pools of reflected light. Where the woods ended and the terraced fields began were the homesteads—straw-thatched huts set amidst gardens of slender areca nut palms and coconut trees. This was one end of the valley across which I had come. The village with its paddy fields encircled the hill on which the temple stood. The hill was a gradual rise on the side from which I had come that ended abruptly where I stood now. On my left the land leveled out to the north-central plains, and I could see the asphalt road, from which I had turned away to cross the paddy fields where people were transplanting, continue. It was rising to leave the valley on a northeasterly course towards where the highland was opening out to low-lying hills. I could see beyond the line of those hills to the distant plains of Raja Rata—The King's Country. On my right was a different land. It was a mass of billowing green rising and falling, wave upon wave, and I was standing there facing the sun on the edge of what seemed like the end of something. There was a blue haze that made the eyes feel tired and want to turn away.

There were footfalls on my back and I turned. The priest came through a cleft in one of the rocks. As he came up he looked more friendly. He walked past me and stood on the edge.

"This point marks one end of the Kandyan Kingdom. From there begins the King's Country." He was pointing vaguely to where the asphalt road was rising through the low hills. "Over to our right beyond the Dumbara Hills is the great plain where the Buddha visited and settled a feud between two tribes. From there right up to the Holy Peak is the abode of God Saman." He began pacing, his rough feet moving easy on the hard rock and his outstretched palm rubbing the bald head, in the way Buddhist priests do. He pointed again to the valley below.

"The old pilgrim path from the King's Country to the Holy Peak went through that village. There are still many travelers' rests all the way to the foot of the Climb."

He used a special Sinhala expression to mean the climb to the Holy Peak. It meant something like "The Holy Trek by the grace of God Saman"—all of it expressed in two simple words, simple when taken separately, but put together giving a sacred ring almost like a temple bell. I thought of Grandmother's trek with her disrobed priest on her pilgrimage of no return.

"Can you see the Peak from here?" It had been a long time since I spoke.

"No. It's on the other side of the range."

I kept looking at the landscape. It had a primeval quality like something at the beginning of time. But the blue haze was flattening the contours and the depth was gone. I wished I had come before the sun became bright. Landscapes are best seen in the gray light of dawn. I heard the Priest's voice. He had said something and I had not been listening.

"Did you say something, Reverend Sir?"

"I said you could see the sea from here at times." I heard him clearly now, and I remained silent. He continued to speak, and his voice seemed pitched to some distance like he was not talking to me.

"Not everyone could see it. If you keep looking straight in a line where I am pointing, you will see a very thin gap between the hills. On a clear day when there are no clouds in the sky, especially after the monsoon rains are over, you may, if you are meritorious enough, see a glint of blue water at the end of that line. Only very few had seen it."

"The Moaning Pond?" I said, and the priest turned around quickly to look at me. For the first time since I saw him there was a faint trace of a smile on his dour face.

"That's what they used to call it in the old days. The Moaning Pond."

I shivered. Was it the cold wind still cutting through the now warming air all the way from the tea country?

"I see it every day now." The priest's voice was once more speaking to a distance. "Since I was a little boy, I would come here at daybreak because I wanted to see the Moaning Pond. I never saw it. Then I donned the yellow robe, and still I watched every morning, and still I saw nothing. I grew old and I couldn't see properly. I had to wear glasses to read. Then one morning I was up before daybreak and meditating here, and the Hour of the Thousand Buddhas came and went and the light touched yonder hills. Then, through that little break in the long line of hills, like through the eye of a needle, I saw the water, blue and glistening like a crest gem. Ever since then I see it. I need glasses to read, but I see faraway things."

I saw Grandmother in white standing on the beach with the waves rising up to her in that long-ago time when we were staying at the bungalow in the rubber estate where Father had taken us. Then I seem to remember something more. Grandmother was telling me how she would come when she was a little girl to the temple on the rock in her village to see the Moaning Pond, because people said if you had collected enough merit in your previous birth you could see the glint of blue water in the break in the mountains, like through the eye of a needle. But she never saw it, not from there. Perhaps the temple in my mind had its genesis in the memory now recalled. But where was it all these years? Was it both true and untrue, like this old priest's vision of the Moaning Pond? Was everything I had recollected and woven together into a tapestry for Asanka as I walked along the riverbank holding her hand something from a secret twilight of my mind?

I never went back to that temple on the rock. I carried it in my mind like the earlier image built upon something Grandmother may have told me. Was the earlier and imagined one different from the one I saw for real? I cannot be sure now. One seemed to have metamorphosed into the other, and now I cannot say which is which. Even the one I carry in my mind now seemed to have changed over the years. Certain details are gone, and there are things in that image now I am not certain were there when I saw the place on that day climbing up along that stairway of rocks with the temple trees on both sides and the path strewn with fallen petals of red and white and then walking into the temple compound of smooth white sand and finally standing on that edge with the land below. I now remember the octagonal roof of an old traveler's rest down below among the terraced rice paddies. In the image I carry in my mind, there is also the white dome of a dagoba far away on the plains beyond the diminishing hills on my left. Were they really there on that day, or are they coming from an earlier memory? How is it that I don't remember coming away from that place? I see the old priest standing on the edge of the rock and drawing lines with an extended arm sweeping across the land from the plains of the King's Country to the mountains in the middle, and then to that faraway haze beyond which the eye wouldn't go. He stands there forever and memory stops with him. Once more there are doubts like I have about most things remembered in this story. But I wish to keep this image of the temple on the rock and an ancient priest standing on the edge that is like the end of something. I have a fear of losing that image, that if ever I went back there it would dissolve like a mirage. Like the vision of the Moaning Pond appearing in the eyes of the half-blind priest who cannot read without glasses but sees only faraway things, the temple on the rock is both true and untrue. Like the earlier image born out of a memory recalled much later, I have followed a grail through time, ever since that day I stood on that rock at the end of the Old Kingdom.

Grandmother's forbears — and through her partly mine — first came across the seas. Seven hundred men, banished from the country of their birth somewhere in the land of the great river Ganga, came in ships and exhausted after many days and nights in the seven seas, threw themselves on the shore and fell asleep. When they woke up, their bodies had turned to the color of copper. It was the sand on which they had lain that gave them the color. Tambapanni — The Land of Copper-Colored

Sand—they named it, and later the sailors of Araby called it Taprobane. The men moved inland and upstream along a waterway that flowed in a southwesterly direction and they named it The River Flowing Through the Valley of Flowers. Their descendants harvested the land and made it bloom and built a great and beautiful city called Anuradhapura. By the third century A.D. they were no longer pirates in exile but civilized men who spoke a beautiful language in which they wrote wonderful poetry, built massive monuments to a religion they had acquired as a gift from the land of their origin—the gentle doctrine of Gotama the Buddha. For a thousand years they ruled the land—the great plains circling around the mountains with the Holy Peak in the center. In them was a reverence for the sea. It was in their songs and their legends. They had come sailing on its waves, and so did their gods and their myths, and they kept the way back to where they came from open, at Mahaththa—The Great Port—which was where their ancestors turned copper.

Suddenly in the eleventh century, for reasons known and unknown, the Sinhalese began leaving the north-central plains. The great cities were abandoned, and the vast reservoirs breached and mangroves choked the irrigation waterways while the people retreated, for over five centuries, to the mountains. For a thousand years they had left the mountains, and the great forests on them, untouched. It was the Thahansi Kele—The Forbidden Forest—where the rains fell and gathered under the trees and the lush tangled undergrowth to flow in streams to water the plains and the fields below. The central highlands were sacred territory, where the great God Saman ruled from the Holy Peak. Now the people were moving into the hidden valleys between the dark and brooding mountains. The sea that brought them to the land was disappearing from view, and the great ports became far away. But they carried with them a vision of the sea as they moved from light to darkness. The sound of waves crashing on the copper-colored beach, where their ancestors first flung themselves, remained a collective memory. They turned the sound into a poetic meter. Most verse in Sinhala, both classical and folk, beginning from the sixteenth century, attempts in its quatrains to simulate the sound of the sea, and hence the name for its meter, *Samudraghosa*, The Sound of the Sea. Like waves, each of the four lines overlap with the next in recitation, until the last line rises sharply in a crescendo to end in a dying fall. It is a sad sound and sung to whichever time has the air of a lament—the woman throwing herself in sorrow or penance. Wrenched and separated from the sea that linked them in a friendly hand-hold to their origin myths over ten centuries, and the freedom of sight and movement of the great plains lost, my grandmother's people of the highlands were further denied, by the white conquerors, access to salt. They boiled raw coconut leaves and wrung the salt-like taste to obtain the basic flavor that would make their food edible. The sea had become a dream, a myth they watered with tears. And so the sad sound, the wailing woman's eternal lament. The Moaning Pond. They would climb the dark mountains, and where they thought they saw the edge of their land where the Moaning Pond lay, they built their temples. The northeast monsoon blew from November to February, and the southwest from March to August. Both winds came across the sea, and having crossed the plains would rain their waters on the slopes of the central highlands. The wind and the rain of those monsoons brought with them the scent of the sea, and then the mountain folk would be overcome with a great longing for going. Like lemmings they pined for the sea.

And so a little girl in the mountains inherited this longing from her ancestors. From the time she could climb the hill in her village, where there was a temple and from where people believed one could see the Moaning Pond if you have done enough merit in your previous birth, she would come to gaze into the distance beyond the mountains of home to the edge of the land where everything was what you thought you saw. She never thought she saw the Moaning Pond from there. Like a migrant bird flying back along the route of some ancestral memory, she reached the sea to "walk the waves" that brought her ancestors to a copper-colored shore and also carried a beautiful princess on its cradle to safety and motherhood.

I see the little girl on that rock where the temple is, gazing towards the west with the rising sun at her back. I see Grandmother, a vision in white standing against the rising waves almost to receive them, unmoved, unafraid. I also see in between, Grandmother leaving the front gate of that split-level house, turning left and moving slowly past the line of fir trees along the asphalt road, looking ahead with head held high, never to return.

And then I am a child once more, of eight going on nine, waiting for her to return from the hills where she has gone to get well.

About the Author

Tissa Abeysekara was born in Colombo, Sri Lanka, in 1939. He began writing fiction in his native Sinhala the late 1950s, but for the next thirty years devoted his professional life to film and television, becoming one of the country's most respected screenwriters and directors. In 1997, at the age of fifty-eight, he published the novella *Bringing Tony Home,* which went on to win Sri Lanka's esteemed Gratiaen Prize, an annual award for the best novel in English given by a trust established by Michael Ondaatje. In addition to many screenplays for television and film, Abeysekara is the author of the novel *In My Kingdom of the Sun and the Holy Peak,* the television series *Pitagamkarayo* ("The Outsiders"), and the collection of short essays *Roots, Reflections & Reminiscences.* He is currently the Director of the Television Training Institute of Sri Lanka.

The Scala International Literature Series

*B*ringing *Tony Home* is published as part of a partnership between North Atlantic Books and Scala House Press.

The mission of the Scala International Literature Series is to publish fiction and literary nonfiction to help develop and foster connections between writers from diverse international cultures and their English-speaking readers around the world. Memoirs, occasional poetry anthologies, and works of literature in this series all seek to explore the qualities that bind and define the human community, while celebrating distinctive traditions and tastes. We are looking for new and original voices, as well as celebrated or neglected works to introduce to English-speaking readers. We are particularly supportive of women's voices. Our publishing goals rest on the premise that good literature, like all good art, has the potential to undermine sectarianism, ideologies, and boundaries that divide us within and outside of national boundaries.

The works we support and celebrate capture the political, historical, personal, or spiritual currents of particular eras and times, drawing out the subtleties of the individual struggle for identity and grace deep within these defining moments.

Other Books in the
Scala International Literature Series

Alamut
A novel by Vladimir Bartol, translated from Slovenian by
Michael Biggins.
$16.95, ISBN 978-1-55643-681-9, 400 pages.

Angels Beneath the Surface
A Selection of Contemporary Slovene Fiction
Edited by Mitja Cănder with Tom Priestly.
$15.95, ISBN 978-1-55643-703-8, 186 pages.

Belonging
New Poetry by Iranians Around the World
Edited by Niloufar Talebi.
$18.95, ISBN 978-1-55643-712-0, 256 pages.

Guarding Hanna
A novel by Miha Mazzini, translated from Slovenian by
Maja Visenjak-Limon.
$15.95, ISBN 978-1-55643-726-7, 272 pages.